THE CHINESE CAT

NOT EVERYONE HAS NINE LIVES…

THE JOHN HAYES THRILLERS
BOOK 10

MARK DAVID ABBOTT

Copyright © 2024 by Mark David Abbott

All rights reserved.

No part of this book may be reproduced in any form or by any electronic or mechanical means, including information storage and retrieval systems, without written permission from the author, except for the use of brief quotations in a book review.

GLOSSARY

Lao wai men (lao wai- singular*)* - Foreigners (Mandarin)

Bao - a type of steamed bun usually with savory fillings (Mandarin)

Jiu Choi Maau - a cat ornament, typically with a waving paw. Believed to bring wealth and good luck. Often seen on shop counters or near the front door of homes.

Bacalhau à Brás. - a Portuguese dish made from shreds of salted cod, onions and thinly chopped fried potatoes, all bound with eggs.

Sim - yes (Portuguese)

Bom dia - Good morning (Portuguese)

Boa tarde - Good afternoon (Portuguese)

Guojia Anquan Bu - Ministry of State Security, China

Obrigado (M)/obrigada (F) - Thank you (Portuguese)

Fai di la - hurry up (Cantonese)

Diu lei lo mo - A very bad swear word in Cantonese that I would rather not translate

1

As dawn crept over Lisbon, Danny Chan unfolded himself from the chair and stretched. He'd been awake most of the night and was glad his shift was finally over. He tipped his head from side to side, stretching out his neck, then clasped his hands behind his back and pulled his shoulders back.

He took one more look into the street below, then walked away from the window and rapped on the bedroom door with the back of his hand.

"Yu-Ming, you're up." He leaned closer to hear the response and when he heard nothing, opened the door and leaned in. "Hey, come on, my shift is over." Danny spoke in English, his command of Mandarin pathetic at best, and Yu-Ming couldn't understand a word of Portuguese.

There was a muffled curse, followed by movement in the darkened room as Yu-Ming rolled out of bed.

"What time is it?" he groaned.

"Time you did some work. Hurry up." Danny left the door open, and walked back to the chair by the window. He picked up his cell phone, typed a brief report, hit send, then slipped it into his back pocket. On a tripod beside the chair was a Canon EOS 5D fitted with a 300 - 600 telephoto lens. He swapped the battery out for a fresh one and put the used one to charge. Finally he checked the parabolic microphone was still picking up sound from the apartment on the other side of the street and that the laptop it was connected to was recording.

Satisfied, he turned around just as Yu-Ming came out of the bedroom.

"You look like shit."

"Well, maybe you should do the night shift for once and then we'll see how great you look," Danny retorted.

"Anything to eat?" Yu-Ming asked, scratching his head and running his eyes over the collection of empty takeaway boxes scattered on the table beside the window.

"Not unless you cooked something."

Yu-Ming shrugged and walked across the small apartment, and stood beside the window, staring out at the opposite building. "Aren't you in a cheery mood this morning?"

"How long are they going to make us sit here, Yu-Ming? It's been over six months. They don't tell us anything. They've reduced the manpower and increased our shifts, and we can't see an end to it."

Yu-Ming sniffed, shrugged, then yawned. "As long as we get paid, who cares?"

Danny scowled. "There's more to life than sitting in this stinking apartment, eating shit food, staring at some *lao wai men's* apartment all day and night. I mean, who are they? She's never there, and all he does is run, drink coffee, and go out in that pretty little car of his. We're wasting our time."

Yu-Ming frowned deeply. "Maybe you should keep your opinions to yourself." He pointed to his ear and then around the apartment.

The Chinese Cat

Danny sneered. "I don't care who's listening. I was born here. They can't send me to China."

Yu-Ming said nothing, his frown and narrowed eyes more than enough to convey his discomfort.

Danny shrugged. He really didn't care. He loved his life in Portugal, had never even been to China, and only spoke a few words of the language to keep his parents happy.

He'd been out of work when the request came through the Chinese community. His father had told him it was important work for the Party. Danny didn't care. He was only interested in the regular pay-check.

But now, after more than six months of utter boredom and terrible hours, he was questioning his choices. The couple across the street seemed like normal people living normal lives, and Danny felt the surveillance was a complete waste of time.

"I'm going home. I'll see you tonight."

"Can you get me some food?"

Danny nodded toward the takeaway menus stuck to the fridge in the kitchen. "Order something. I'm going home to sleep."

"I can't take this *lao wai* food anymore. Can you bring me something from home? Some of your mother's *bao*?"

Danny grinned. Sometimes, he felt sorry for Yu-Ming. It wouldn't have been easy to come straight from China to a foreign country and spend the whole time in a flat living on takeaway food.

There had been another guy too, for the first three months, so he'd had some company at the beginning, but that guy had been called back and now there were just the two of them. A man from China who had never traveled abroad before, and Danny, who was of Chinese descent but spoke Portuguese and English fluently, with very little knowledge of Mandarin.

"I'll bring you something if you take the early part of my shift."

Yu-Ming nodded eagerly. "Some *bao* or even those noodles she made last time."

Danny nodded. "I'll ask her. I'm out of here." He jerked his head toward the street. "Have fun watching the *lao wai* make coffee."

2

John slowed his pace to a fast walk, his heart still racing from his run. Glancing down at his watch, he grinned. He'd knocked a minute off his best time. He flashed a smile at an elderly lady walking her pug and continued walking while he regained his breath. The cool morning air filled his lungs as he savored the familiar rush of endorphins.

The sun was still low in the sky, painting the buildings in hues of amber and gold and throwing long shadows across the cobblestones. Apart from the elderly lady and her dog, he had the street to himself.

Nearing the corner, he paused and gazed up into the plane trees, alive with the sound of blackbirds, starlings, and sparrows, chattering and squawking as they, too, began their day.

John loved the early morning. It had its own energy—calm and filled with promise. Combined with the endorphins from hard exercise, it made him feel on top of the world.

The last seven months had passed in a whirlwind of

activity, but his regular morning run helped give him peace of mind and the strength to deal with whatever the universe threw at him.

Once a month, he'd made the long drive from Lisbon to Winchester in England to check on the rebuilding of his parents' house. It was a two-day journey, and would have been quicker to fly, but John enjoyed being out on the road in his Porsche 911 T. The little sports car was over fifty years old but had the heart and lungs of a teenager and he relished putting it through its paces, avoiding the motorways and taking the more challenging country roads.

He was leaving again tomorrow, but this time Adriana was coming with him. The thought made him smile. His parents loved her. They had loved Charlotte too, and at first John was apprehensive they would always compare Adriana to her. But he needn't have worried. His dad, a grumpy, taciturn man at the best of times, transformed when she was around, laughing and chatting about all manner of subjects. His mum was particularly fond of her too, and often made unsubtle hints about making the relationship permanent.

A steel shutter rattled open across the street, breaking his chain of thought, and he glanced over at the owner opening up his café. For a brief moment, John contemplated popping in for a coffee, but it would take time for the owner to set up, and John could make one at home just the way he liked it.

He entered the lobby of his apartment building and waved a greeting to the security guard.

"*Bom dia, Senhor* Hayes."

"*Bom dia*, João." John's smile faded, and for a moment was unable to speak, but he quickly regained control. Walking over to the counter, he leaned casually on the top and forced a smile. "When did you get that?"

João shrugged. "It was here when I started my shift."

John frowned. "I don't remember seeing it yesterday."

"No, I think Miguel must have brought it in during the night shift. He likes these things. Believes in... how do you say... feng sway?"

"*Fung Shui*," John corrected him, pronouncing it in the Cantonese way.

"*Fung Shui*," João repeated, then shrugged and smiled at the same time. "It doesn't matter to me. If it brings good luck, who am I to say no?"

John faked a smile. "Yes, agreed, well... have a good day, João."

"You too, *Senhor* Hayes."

John turned away, walking over toward the bank of elevators. He pressed the button and cast a glance over his shoulder at the counter, as an uneasy feeling replaced the buzz from his run. The elevator chimed its arrival, and he gave his head a shake, took a deep breath and stepped inside. Pressing the button for his floor, he stepped back in to the rear of the elevator and leaned against the handrail, his eyes on the numbers as they counted upwards.

It was probably nothing, he told himself.... No, it was nothing.

He took another deep breath and stepped forward as the elevator reached his floor, and the doors opened. He walked down the corridor, punched in the entry code to his apartment, and stepped inside.

"Good morning, *querido*. Good run?" Adriana was already sitting at the breakfast bar, dressed for work. She had her iPad in front of her and John could see a news feed playing on the screen.

"Superb. Beat my time this morning." He slipped off his

running shoes, walked across the apartment, wrapped his arms around her and kissed her on the top of her head.

"Ewww, you're all sweaty," Adriana protested half-heartedly.

He released his hold, but she grabbed his hand and held on, swiveling on her stool to face him. Her eyes searched his face, and he forced his smile wider, not wanting his uneasiness to show.

She frowned slightly. "Is everything okay?"

He could never hide anything from her. "Yes, I'm... just a bit preoccupied about the trip tomorrow."

Adriana squeezed his hand. "I'm looking forward to it. That reminds me, I promised to take a bottle of Port for your dad. I'll pick it up during my lunch break. Graham's is his favorite, right?"

"Yes, but to be honest, you could get him anything and he'd be happy."

Adriana chuckled. "It's better I get the one he likes." Her eyes traced the contours of his face. "You should be proud of what you've done in such a short time. To get their house rebuilt so quickly."

John shrugged, let go of her hand, and walked around the counter until he was facing her. "I've had a lot of help."

"Yes, but still. Your parents are very impressed."

John's eyes strayed to the French press.

"I've just made it," Adriana answered the unspoken question. "The way you taught me."

John grinned. Adriana used to tease him about weighing the beans before grinding and timing the brew. But now she did it as well. He poured himself a cup, held it in both hands, and inhaled the steam rising from the cup.

Adriana watched him expectantly. "Good?"

John took a sip and gave an approving nod of his head. "Very good. The student has become the master."

Adriana giggled, then climbed off the stool and picked up her iPad. "Well, the master has to go. I've got a lot of work to finish today if we're going to be away for the next week." She leaned over the counter and John leaned forward to kiss her on the lips.

"I'll see you this evening."

John watched her walk across the apartment, open the door and turn back to wave goodbye. He smiled, but all he could see was the *Fung Shui* cat on the guard's counter down in the lobby, waving its right paw at him.

3

John couldn't take his mind off the cat.

Known as a *Jiu Choi Maau*, a "good fortune" cat, it was anything but, in John's mind.

John had been away in England when a *Jiu Choi Maau* had been left inside his locked apartment in Lisbon while Adriana was asleep.

[1]It had been a message from Xie Longwei, the neighbor who was terrorizing his parents. A display of his power and reach.

In the end, Xie's attempt at intimidation hadn't done him any good. Sipping his coffee, John's gaze drifted across the Lisbon skyline as he recalled Xie being bundled into an unmarked helicopter by Joseph Tamba and his men, before being flown back to the Democratic Republic of Nkuru. Xie had been blackmailing Joseph's father, the President of Nkuru, for personal gain and to expand the influence of the Chinese Communist Party over the country.

Was Xie still alive? Or was he rotting in an African prison?

Either way, Xie had been dealt with, so John wondered why he was so troubled by the sight of the cat.

It was probably a coincidence. In fact, it had to be.

He shook his head and turned away from the window. Paranoia. That's all it was.

---

1. See "The Neighbor: John Hayes #9"

4

After a leisurely breakfast and several cups of coffee, John spent the morning preparing the car for the long journey ahead.

The vintage Porsche had been fully restored and modernised, but that didn't mean John took it for granted. He checked the oil and fluid levels and adjusted the tire pressures. The tread on the rears was getting low, and he made a mental note to change them when he got back. He also gave the windscreen a thorough clean, both inside and out, and checked his driving glasses and gloves were in the glove box. He had made the journey back to England multiple times over the past few months, so the pre-journey check had become a matter of routine, but John enjoyed it. Ensuring his pride and joy was kept in tip-top running order gave him immense pleasure.

Finally, happy everything was as it should be, he took the car for a quick blast in the Sintra Mountains west of Lisbon. He told himself it was to make sure everything was running properly, but the reality was he relished being behind the wheel. The Porsche was built for pure driving pleasure and he used it every opportunity he could get. It also, just like running, allowed him time to empty his mind, to enter a flow state as he worked his way up and down the gears, finding the perfect line through a corner, positioning his right foot correctly to heel and toe on the downshifts, blipping the throttle to match the revs.

Just outside Sintra, he pulled over beside a little roadside café and climbed out. He stood for a moment on the pavement, looking down at the Bahia Red sports car, hearing the ticking of the engine as it cooled, and sighed a happy sigh.

"*Carro bonito!*"

John turned and smiled at the elderly man in a crisp white apron standing in the café's doorway.

"*Obrigado.*" John removed his driving glasses and glanced at his watch. He was hungry. "Am I too early for lunch?"

"No, no, please make yourself comfortable. I'll bring you a menu."

John chose a table outside, sat down, and stretched out his legs.

The elderly man arrived with a menu and said, "I recommend the *Bacalhau à Brás*. The *Bacalhau* is fresh this morning."

John handed the menu back. "Done. And I'll have a *Vinho Verde*. Do you have *Quinta da Aveleda*?"

"*Sim.*"

"I'll have a glass of that."

"Excellent choice, *Senhor.*" The man paused. "You speak very good Portuguese for an Englishman."

John chuckled. "But obviously not good enough to pass as a local."

The man shrugged. "Close enough. It was some of the

pronunciation that gave it away. But I'm impressed you made the effort to learn. Many don't."

John shrugged. "It's my home now. It's the least I can do."

The man smiled and placed a hand on John's shoulder. "I'll bring your wine."

John leaned back in his chair enjoying the warm sun on his face. He could hear voices inside the café, but so far, he was the only one sitting outside.

A woman passed by, holding shopping bags in each hand. She briefly looked at the car, then at the café. John caught her eye, and she nodded a greeting. Across the street, two boys in school uniforms were excitedly talking and pointing at the Porsche. They stopped at the curb, looked both ways, and then quickly crossed the street to stand beside the car. John listened in on their conversation.

"It's a Ferrari. It's red."

"No, you idiot, it's a Porsche. German."

The café owner appeared beside John and placed a glass of *Vinho Verde* on the table. "Why aren't you in school?" he called out and the two boys stopped their banter, looked guiltily at him and then John, then hurried away down the footpath.

The old man smiled down at John. "Those were the best days."

"Hmmm." John didn't really agree. He actually preferred being an adult. Adults made their own decisions and got to do amazing things, like driving a classic Porsche on winding roads and stopping for lunch at a quaint café. He reached for the wine, noticing the beads of condensation running down the side of the glass.

"The first one is on the house."

John blinked in surprise, then raised the glass and toasted the owner. "*Muito obrigado.*"

He waited until the owner had gone back inside before taking a sip. The wine was excellent—crisp and clean, with citrus undertones and a touch of green fruit—although he would have preferred it slightly more chilled.

His life had changed drastically since he had left England for the first time. From his first overseas posting in India, and the tragedy that befell the love of his life, to living in Hong Kong, Thailand, and now Portugal.

But everything that had happened to him, good or bad, had made him the man he was now. No longer innocent and naive, but stronger, more confident... and maybe a bit cynical. He still believed in the underlying goodness of his fellow man, but knew that life wasn't always bunny rabbits and fluffy pillows. There was loss, heartbreak, and evil out there, but also love, friendship, and generosity. Just like the old man who had given him a free glass of wine.

John thought about his parents. Evil and greed had destroyed their home, but kindness and generosity were getting it rebuilt. The city councillor, Philip Symonds had fast-tracked the permits, his friend Will had referred a specialist contractor, and helped with some of the work, and a neighboring farmer had provided a cottage for his parents to live in for a reduced rate until their home was finished.

John felt something brush against his leg and looked down to see a ginger cat rubbing against him. He reached down to pat it and an image of the *Jiu Choi Maau* flashed across his mind. He frowned as he ran his hand along the cat's back, the cat arching its spine and purring with pleasure.

It might be paranoia, but he would still ask the guard on the night-shift where it came from.

5

Wang Mingmei slammed the laptop closed, shut her eyes and counted to ten. She had kept her emotions in check during the video conference call, but now it had ended, she was struggling to maintain her composure.

Why didn't they understand? All she wanted was some more time and their support.

Xie Longwei was... she felt a lump in her throat—she refused to believe he was dead—Xie Longwei *is* a great man. He had done more for the Party than anyone she knew, and yet they were prepared to forget about him as if he had never existed.

Conflicting emotions raged within her. Anger at their callousness and lack of support, but also a deep sense of loss.

She missed him every day. For almost twenty years she had worked for Xie and had grown to respect him deeply. She had always maintained a professional relationship and had never told him the depth of her feelings. But that was something she regretted now.

His disappearance had left a deep hole in her life. A deep hole she filled with thoughts of revenge. But she would bring him back and then punish those responsible..

That awful night was etched in her memory. The gunfire, the panicked shouts from her security team, the explosions. She had just managed to escape the office when the unknown men in black had thrown the stun grenades in. The blast had disoriented her even though she was outside, and by the time she got her bearings, the shooting was all over. Stumbling through the darkness, she had made her way around the stable block offices and into the main house through a side entrance. But when she got there, Xie was gone.[1]

Her heart rate had spiked at the memory and once more she closed her eyes and took several deep breaths. She prided herself on never showing emotion, and even though she was alone in the hotel room, she still fought to keep everything under control.

She was convinced the *lao wai,* Hayes, was behind it all, and she had thrown her energies into proving it and tracking Xie down. But after six months of surveillance, she was no further forward.

There had been crumbs, hints, whispers, but nothing concrete. Her gut told her there was also an African connection, which was why she was currently holed up in a hotel in Zalendi, the capital of Nkuru. It was whispered that Xie was being held in a secret prison in the capital, but so far, she had found no evidence that it was true.

After six months, and nothing to show for it, the *Guojia Anquan Bu* was withdrawing support. They had already cut back her surveillance team to a couple of inexperienced men, but now they had given her until the end of the week to pull the plug completely.

She stood and walked over to the window and gazed out over the multi-colored roofs of the city. It was market day, and the streets teemed with people. Street vendors lined the sides of the roads hawking vegetables, meat... and, ironically, cheap plastic items from China. The sight filled her with little pleasure.

Mingmei was gambling on one last roll of the dice. Something she had planned meticulously. She had funded it herself, and kept everyone on a need-to-know basis. Even her superiors were unaware.

Because they would never sanction what she had planned.

---

1. See "The Neighbor: John Hayes #9"

6

John blinked his eyes open and for a moment struggled to figure out where he was. He was in a car but couldn't remember why or where he was heading.

Adriana was beside him and she smiled before turning her attention back to the road ahead. "Good nap?"

John frowned and thought about the question.

"Are you okay?" Adriana glanced over again, her eyebrows raised.

"Yeah, yeah." John sighed and rubbed his face. "Just a bit groggy. How long was I out for? Where are we?"

Adriana glanced in the mirror, then over at the map on the iPhone on the dashboard. "About twenty minutes from your parents' place."

"Wow, so I've slept for..." he did a quick calculation, "almost two hours."

"And you were snoring."

"Huh." John shifted his position in his seat and rotated his shoulders. "Do you want me to take over?"

"No." She shook her head. "I'm okay."

John lapsed back into silence, the grogginess from his sleep still clouding his brain. He hadn't realized how tired he was. He usually made the trip by himself, splitting the journey into two days, the night stop enough for him to recharge his batteries. But this time, it was as if his body knew he could take a break and let someone else drive.

He watched Adriana, as she downshifted for a bend, expertly matching the revs with a blip off the throttle, before placing her hands back at a quarter-to-three on the wheel. He smiled.

"Enjoying yourself?"

Adriana chuckled. "I love this car."

"Yeah," he sighed. He knew what she meant. It wasn't the latest design, and the technology was over fifty years old, but the car had character, and if you loved driving, there was no other car that gave as much feedback, making you feel as if you and the car were one. There was a reason the Porsche 911 design had endured for so long.

It was the first time Adriana had driven over with him, and he was glad she had taken the time to do so. There was something about sharing a long road trip with someone, especially someone you love. It helped that she was a skilled driver, too. When he had first bought the car, he had been nervous about letting her behind the wheel. He had never been a good passenger, but he relaxed within minutes as she piloted the car with the ease of a racing driver.

"You never told me where you learnt to drive so well," John broke the silence.

Adriana smiled, but took her time to answer. She downshifted, gave a quick toot of the horn, and then pulled out to overtake a slower moving car. She waited until she was safely back on her side of the road before grinning at John.

"An ex-boyfriend."

The Chinese Cat

John cocked an eyebrow. "Ah, so that's why you didn't tell me," he said in mock disdain. "I hate him already."

Adriana's grin widened. "He was a professional racing driver for a few years."

"I hate him even more."

Adriana looked over at him, and her grin faltered. "Are you jealous?"

"Very."

She went quiet.

John let her suffer for a minute and then laughed. "Of course not. Why would I be jealous? In fact, I'm happy he taught you to drive so well." He placed a reassuring hand on her arm. "Why do you think I slept so long? I'm a terrible passenger. I don't trust anyone."

Adriana nodded, but the smile had left her face.

John moved his hand to her thigh, giving it a squeeze. "Hey, I'm serious. We're adults, not teenagers. We've both had relationships before. Hell, I was married, remember?"

She nodded again, her eyes still on the road.

"I love you, Adriana, more than anything in the world."

"More than this car?" Adriana was smiling again.

"Well... I wouldn't go that far."

7

"Here?"

"The gate ahead on the left." John pointed through the windshield.

Adriana slowed, then turned left between the gateposts, the car rumbling across the cattle grid.

"It's beautiful around here," she said as she gazed around at the farmland stretching out on either side of the farm track.

John grunted agreement. It was. Lush green fields as far as they could see and majestic old oak and sycamore trees that lined the road like ancient watchmen.

"Look over there." He pointed to his right.

He heard a sharp intake of breath from Adriana, and the car slowed to a stop. "Is that...?"

"Fallow deer. There's a lot around here."

"Wild?"

"Yes." John nodded. "But not native. The Normans brought them over about a thousand years ago."

"Beautiful."

John considered her face for a long moment. *She* was

beautiful. Thick dark hair tumbled onto her shoulders, her skin lightly tanned from the Portuguese sun. With her dark Ray-Bans, she looked like she should be on the cover of Vogue rather than sitting beside him.

"What are you looking at, Mr. Hayes?"

John smiled and shrugged.

The corners of her mouth quirked in a smile, then she released the clutch and the car moved forward.

"See the cottage on the right? That's where they're staying until the house is finished."

"It looks so... English. I mean ... in a good way. Like something out of Pride and Prejudice."

"Yes, we were lucky to get this. It's very close to Willow Cottage, so the area is familiar. Dad doesn't like change. He gets grumpy."

"He's never grumpy with me."

John laughed. "No, you can't do anything wrong in his eyes."

"It's my Portuguese charm."

"It sure is. It won me over." John pointed at the blue Ford Focus parked in front of the small stone cottage. "Just park behind that. I'll sort the parking out later."

As Adriana pulled in behind the Focus and turned the engine off, the front door opened and first David Hayes appeared in the doorway, then Carole. Adriana waved through the windshield, then unbuckled her seatbelt and climbed out.

John stayed put, watching as Adriana met his parents halfway down the pathway, throwing her arms around his father, giving him a tight hug, before doing the same to his mother. John smiled as the three of them stood together talking excitedly, completely forgetting John was there.

A warmth spread through his body, and his eyes moistened. "Come on John Hayes," he muttered. "You're getting sentimental."

Unbuckling his seatbelt, he opened the door and climbed out, stretching out the kinks from the long drive.

"John, dear, what are you dawdling for? Come on in and freshen up before lunch."

"Lunch? Mum, it's so late. I told you we'd eat on the way."

"Nonsense." She dismissed him with a wave of her hand. "We've been waiting for you. Now hurry up."

Adriana had pushed her sunglasses onto the top of her head and had her arm looped inside his father's. She grinned. "Yes, come on John, hurry up."

John shook his head in mock exasperation, then caught his father's eye.

His father nodded back. "John."

"Dad."

Then the three of them turned toward the house, leaving John to follow. He hesitated, glancing back at the car, then decided to get their bags later, and followed them up the path, casting his eye around the garden as he did so.

There were always a few things for him to do when he visited, but this time the lawn was freshly mowed and the flowerbeds looked like they had been recently tilled.

"Who's doing the garden for you?" he called out as he removed his shoes at the door.

"A boy from the farm," John's father replied from the other end of the hallway.

But John didn't hear him. The sight of something on the mantelpiece in the living room sucked the air from his lungs, and he froze.

When John didn't reply or move, David Hayes asked, "John? Are you okay?"

John blinked. "Ah... yeah."

"Come on, son. I'm starving, but your mum wouldn't let me eat until you arrived."

John took a breath and followed him into the kitchen. The small kitchen table was laid for four and Adriana was helping his mum to heat the food.

David Hayes sat down and looked at John quizzically. "Are you alright, son? You look like you've seen a ghost."

John grunted, then walked over to the sink to wash his hands. Turning on the tap, he ran cold water over his hands, then cleared his throat. "Um... the ahhh... Chinese cat on the mantelpiece. That wasn't there last time."

"Do you like it, John? It must remind you of Hong Kong," his mum replied brightly. "Gladys gave it to me. She said it brings good luck. Feng sway, she said."

"*Fung Shui.*" John turned the tap off, looked around for a dishtowel, then dried his hands, his forehead creased in a deep frown. What was it with seeing these damn cats everywhere? He sighed heavily, then looped the dishtowel over the cabinet door handle. Coincidence. That's all it was. Not only was he sentimental, but paranoid, too. He took another deep breath, fixed a broad smile on his face, then walked over to the table and sat down.

"Actually, Mum, I'm glad you waited for us," he announced. "I'm starving."

8

"I have to check on the cottage this morning."

"Can I come with you?"

John smiled. "Of course, why not?"

Adriana shrugged, wiped her mouth with her napkin, then set it down beside her plate. "I don't want to get in the way."

"Don't worry," John chuckled. "I'm sure you'll provide the builders with a welcome distraction." He turned to his father, who was slurping on a cup of tea.

"Are you coming, Dad?"

He shook his head. "Not this morning, son. We were there a couple of days ago."

John nodded. "Is there anything you want me to deal with while I'm there?"

David Hayes smiled. "No, it's all going well." He put his teacup down and glanced at Carole. "I know we've said it before, son, but thank you for everything you're doing for us."

John's mum reached over and placed a hand over John's. "Yes dear. Thank you. We're so blessed to have a son like you."

John's cheeks flushed, and he glanced self consciously at Adriana before looking down at his breakfast plate. He shrugged. "It's... well, the least I could do. I couldn't leave you to deal with it by yourself." Feeling uncomfortable, he pushed back his chair and stood up. "I'll do the dishes and then we'll go."

"No, John, leave the dishes to me," his mother protested.

Adriana pushed her chair back too and picked up her plate. "Not at all, Carole. You made us this lovely breakfast. It's the least we can do."

Carole flashed her a broad smile. "Okay, I won't argue."

John rolled up his sleeves and turned on the kitchen tap. "If Dad's not coming, why don't we walk over?" He looked out the kitchen window. "It's a lovely morning."

"Yes." Adriana joined him beside the sink. "It does look nice." She leaned in and kissed him on the cheek, then went back to the table and began clearing the breakfast dishes.

Thirty minutes later, John stood on the pathway in front of the house as Adriana sat on the top step and laced up her running shoes.

The sky was almost clear, just a few clouds punctuating the blue, and the air was clean and crisp. A pair of sparrows chirped from their perch on the cottage roof before flying off, and several butterflies flitted from flower to flower in the garden. John took a deep breath and exhaled slowly, a deep sense of contentment filling his body.

"You seem happier here," she said.

John raised an eyebrow. "Happier?"

"Yes, more at home."

He stuck out his lip and shrugged, then glanced around the garden, wondering what he should say.

Adriana stood and brushed the dust off the seat of her

jeans before walking closer and linking her arm through his.

"Do you want to move back?"

"No, no, not at all." John frowned and shook his head. "I'm very happy where we are."

"Okay." But it sounded like she didn't believe him.

John led the way down the path, past the two parked cars and out the front gate, thinking about what she had said. He felt he should say something.

"I wouldn't say I'm happier here. It's just… familiar."

He gave her a reassuring smile. "I grew up here, remember?"

She smiled back, but her eyes were searching his face.

He pulled her closer, then unlinked his arm and wrapped it around her and gave her a tight squeeze. "Don't worry, I'm not planning to come back here. It's not home anymore. My home is wherever you are." He tipped his head and kissed her on the forehead. His words seemed to have reassured her because she squeezed him back and then changed the subject.

"So how far away is their cottage?"

"As the crow flies, not far. I know some shortcuts."

"How?"

"When I was a kid, I used to roam these fields. This farm is actually very close to the old Atwell Estate, where my parents have their cottage."

He led her down the farm track toward the main road, but before getting there, stopped beside a stile set in the hedgerow that bordered the track.

"Over here."

He held Adriana's hand as she climbed over, then hopped over the stile, landing easily in the next field. He pointed at a yellow arrow on the post beside the stile. "See this. This means it's a public footpath. There have probably been people walking this way for centuries."

Adriana nodded and gazed out across the field as it sloped gently away from them. A small herd of cattle stared at them curiously from a distant corner.

"We have something similar in Portugal. They're called *caminho rural*."

"Yes, I've heard of that." John gestured across the field. "This way."

They walked slowly, enjoying the morning sun and the tranquil countryside, comfortable in each other's company.

After some time, Adriana broke the silence. "You know, if you want to spend more time with your parents, don't let me get in the way. I mean, I know they're getting older and..." she trailed off.

John looked at her curiously. "Why do you keep talking like this?"

"Well," she shrugged and averted her gaze, "I mean..." She looked back at him, her face suddenly serious. "We live in my country, my parents are in the same place, I speak the language... It's unfair for me to expect you to stay there."

John laughed. "Hey, I don't know what's got into you this morning." He stopped and turned to face her. "Look, I've lived away from home since the moment I was old enough. I've lived in India, Thailand, Hong Kong, and now with you in Portugal. It's my choice. You're not forcing me to do anything." He waved his arm to encompass the fields. "As beautiful as this is, I don't want to move back." He shrugged and grinned at the same time. "What makes me value this time with my parents is that I don't see them all the time. And I think that makes them value it, too." He shook his head. "My dad thinks the world of you, so you've only ever seen him in a good mood. But trust me, he can be a grumpy old git and he drives me nuts if I spend too much time with him."

Adriana looked down at the ground and kicked at the grass with the toe of her running shoe.

"Trust me, I don't want to spend all my time here," John continued, reaching for her hand. "I have my life, they have theirs. And that's the way it will continue. I'll be there whenever they need it, but I have my own life to lead."

Adriana looked up again, her eyes roaming his face.

"Why are you suddenly so insecure? You're normally so confident and secure in yourself."

She shrugged. "I... I don't know. I... I... forget it. It doesn't matter. I think I just woke up in a strange mood."

John held her gaze, then smiled and tugged her hand. "Come on, let's go and see the cottage. That will cheer you up. I think you'll be surprised at how much they've done since the last time you were here."

9

Chow Yun-long lowered the binoculars and licked his lips. The familiar rush before action vibrated through his system. Turning back to the white Ford Transit van, he raised a gloved hand and gave a thumbs up.

The man behind the steering wheel nodded and started the engine.

Chow walked back to the van, slid the side door back, and climbed in.

"Now?"

"Now," Chow replied to the young man seated on the floor in the back of the van.

The young man grinned in a flash of white teeth and slapped his thigh. "About fucking time."

Chow nodded and dropped to his knees on the floor of the van as it edged forward, moving slowly down the farm track toward the road. He could feel the adrenaline building and he slowed his breathing, long deep breaths through his nostrils as he stowed the binoculars in the black kitbag beside him.

The other man, Wang Jun, was pulling on a black balaclava and then twisted his head from side to side, limbering up his neck.

"Remember, we need to be quick. No heroics."

"I know, I know," the young man replied, a trace of impatience creeping into his voice.

The older man frowned slightly, studying his young colleague for a moment, then returned his attention to his own equipment. From the bag, he removed a balaclava and pulled it onto his head, leaving it rolled until the last minute. He then removed a small canvas pouch from the kit bag and unzipped it, revealing an auto-injector which he slid into the side pocket of his black tactical pants. Finally he removed a bundle of zip-ties and velcroed them in place on the front of his load vest.

The van lurched and then turned right, the going becoming smoother as it joined the road and increased speed.

Chow took another long, deep breath and sat back on his heels.

Wang kneeled in front of him, his eyes wide, unable to conceal his excitement.

Chow hadn't worked with him before, but Wang had come highly recommended. Chow didn't enjoy working with the young guys. They were often too eager to prove themselves, and took unnecessary risks, or worst still, didn't follow instructions.

"Exactly as we rehearsed," Chow reminded him, and the young man failed to hide the irritation in his expression. He nodded, but didn't say anything, his eyes flicking toward the front of the van.

"I see them," the driver spoke and the van slowed.

Chow glanced at Wang again.

The Chinese Cat

At the news from the driver, the young man shifted into a crouch and turned to face the side door. He gripped the door handle with one hand, bracing himself, while the other hand moved toward his belt.

Chow pushed himself to his feet, ducking his head only slightly to avoid the roof, one of the few times he was grateful for his lack of height. He leaned back against the side of the van and braced himself while turning to look out the windshield. He could see them now, walking side by side along the edge of the road. The man had a hand on the woman's opposite shoulder and they appeared to be deep in conversation.

The man heard the van approaching, and stepped behind the woman, easing her closer to the road edge, while following her in single file.

Chow's team had chosen the van for its anonymity, white Ford vans a common sight on English roads, so he didn't expect any problems. But he still didn't want to lose the element of surprise.

"Go, go, go," he urged, and the driver accelerated, closing the gap in seconds.

Chow watched Wang stand, hunched against the roof, his hand still on the lock while the other unclipped a metal baton from his load belt and he spread his feet, bracing himself for the vehicle stopping

The van lurched to a halt and the side door slid open, Wang leaping out and raising his right arm all in one movement.

10

"How much longer do you think it will take?"

"About ten minutes," John replied as he helped Adriana over another stile and down onto the road. "We just have to follow the road for about five hundred metres, then take a left."

"Ha, no," Adriana laughed. "I meant the rebuilding."

"Ah." John smiled at his mistake. He rested his left hand on her shoulder as they walked up the road. "Well, the new windows went in last week, so that's all the exterior work done. The plumbing is completed, and the wiring will get done now the house is weathertight."

"Okay..." Adriana looked over at him and grinned. "That still doesn't answer my question."

"No." John grinned back. "I suppose it doesn't." He reached up and tucked a stray lock of hair behind her ear, then placed his hand back on her shoulder and gave it a squeeze. "A couple of months, I guess."

"It's been pretty fast."

"Yes, I've been lucky. We had a good team. All thanks to Philip and Will."

"Will they be there now?"

John turned his wrist to look at his watch. "Will said he'd be there."

"Okay."

Without Philip and Will, the repairs would have taken much longer, and he wouldn't have had the confidence to run the project remotely from Portugal. But it had all gone smoothly and his parents were getting a much improved, modernised house, and even a stair-lift for the future when they couldn't manage the stairs. He smiled and nodded to himself.

The movement caught Adriana's attention. "What?"

"Nothing, I was just thinking that everything works out alright in the end."

"Hmmm."

Before Adriana could say more, John heard an approaching vehicle, and he looked back over his shoulder.

He stepped back behind Adriana, and gently eased her closer to the side of the road, making sure his body was between hers and the oncoming van.

"You sound like you don't agree?" he continued.

"No, it's not that, it's just..."

John noticed the engine note of the van increasing as if it was speeding up. He frowned and looked back over his shoulder. It was a plain white transit van, nothing unusual, but the hair on the back of his neck tingled a warning. His frown deepened, but he tuned back into Adriana's conversation, convincing himself he was being paranoid again.

"...sometimes don't turn out for the best. Look at..."

John had tuned out again, realising the van was approaching at high speed. He looked back over his shoulder, his grip on Adriana's shoulder tightening. She stopped speaking, realising something was wrong, and they both halted as the van screeched to a stop beside them.

The van door slid open, and a person dressed in black jumped out. John instinctively pushed Adriana away from him and raised his right arm as the long object in the black figure's hand came down toward him. He took most of the blow on his forearm, deflecting it to the side. Time seemed to slow down as he struggled to grasp what was happening. His arm throbbed, and his fingers wouldn't move. Meanwhile, another figure in black, concealed under a balaclava, jumped out of the van and headed towards Adriana, who was sprawled in the grass beside the road. John's mind snapped back into focus, and he moved towards her, determined to protect her. A blow to his head knocked him sideways, setting his ears ringing and turning everything black. When his vision cleared, he found himself lying half on the road and half in the hedgerow. His head throbbed with pain, but he must have been out for only a second because he could see the person in black leaning over Adriana as she tried to scramble away. The figure had something in his hand, and he slammed it into her thigh.

John forced himself out of the long grass, the movement sending a wave of nausea running through him. His vision blurred, and he struggled to regain his balance. Another blow struck across his shoulders and he collapsed back into the grass. A boot found his ribs, forcing the air from his lungs, then another blow found the back of his head. Struggling once more to rise, his brain failed to send signals to his body. Through stars he saw Adriana get picked up, her struggles becoming weaker and then thrown into the van. Her assailant climbed in after her, leaving John's attacker looming over him. There was a shout from the van, but John's scrambled brain couldn't make sense of it. His attacker raised the long object again as if to strike him once more, when John heard another shout and the attacker hesitated, then backed away before climbing back into the van and sliding the door shut.

With a chirp of the tires, the van pulled away, just as John's vision went black again.

11

"John, John... hey... John, wake up... he's not responding."

John could hear the words, but couldn't work out what he was supposed to do.

"John..."

Pain increased in intensity.

"Should I call an ambulance?" It was another voice, different from the first.

The pain expanded faster and faster, then exploded, filling his head with a flash of intense white light, a ringing reverberating through his skull, and he groaned.

"John..."

Through the pain, he felt fingers tapping the side of his face, and he blinked his eyes open. There was light and blurred objects. He blinked again, and his vision cleared. A man looked down at him, his head close to John's, his face creased with worry. He looked familiar.

"John... what happened to you? You look like you've been hit by a car."

"Should I call an ambulance?" the other voice asked again.

John couldn't see who it was.

The man, looking down at him, shook his head. "Wait..."

Then it all came back and John pushed the man away, fighting to get to his feet. The effort sent pain searing through his body and redoubled the ringing in his head. Nausea filled his system, and he leaned over and dry retched. Spitting on the road, he looked past the man leaning over him... where was she? His eyes darted around, searching for her, the movement of his eyeballs sending shafts of pain through his skull.

"A... Adriana...." he gasped.

"Adriana?"

John looked back at the man. He finally registered who it was. Will Sanderson, his contractor.

"Someone took her..." John struggled to get up, but gave up as the contents of his stomach threatened to make a reappearance in his mouth.

"John, slow down... what happened?"

John's mind raced, running back over the events. "A white van... two men in black... kidnap..." He again tried to get up, this time succeeding in getting into a sitting position. He looked up the road. "They went that way."

"Fuck," Will growled. He glared up the road, then turned to look at the young man beside him, one of his workers. "Paul, call the police. Tell them to get down here as soon as possible. Tell them a woman's been assaulted and kidnapped."

He looked back at John, his eyes roaming John's face, "and you'd better ask for an ambulance."

John shook his head and winced. "No...no." He grabbed Will's arm. "Help me up..."

Will hesitated.

"Now!"

Will stood, then reached down and pulled John to his feet. Will was a big man, and it was easy enough for him to do, but the movement completely disoriented John and he clung to Will for support. John gasped, blinking rapidly to clear his vision, then straightened up. Pain radiated from the right side of his head and he reached up, probing the side of his head with his fingertips. There was something sticky and just the touch of his fingertips sent more pain radiating through his skull. He took a deep breath and pain lanced through his ribcage.

"We have to go after her," he said feebly. "Give me your keys."

Will stepped back, his head tilted to one side, frowning deeply.

"Give me your keys," John repeated and stepped forward, almost losing his balance.

Will steadied him and shook his head. "You're in no state to drive, John. You need to go to the hospital."

"Fuck the hospital," John roared, anger and frustration overriding the pain. "Give me your keys."

Will shook his head then, realising John wouldn't give up, replied, "Okay, but I'll drive, come on."

He took John's arm, draped it over his shoulder, then led him back toward his Mitsubishi Pajero. He helped John climb inside, then ran around to the driver's side and opened the door.

Paul removed the phone from his ear and protested, "The cops... the ambulance...they're coming."

"Wait for them," Will called out, slammed the door and put the SUV in gear. He glanced over at John, then stamped on the accelerator and roared away up the road.

12

"Faster, Will, faster." John sat forward in his seat, no seat belt, his hands gripping the grab handle on the dashboard. "They're getting away."

Will shot him a quick glance, then returned his attention to the narrow country road, pounding the horn as they rounded blind corners at speed.

"John, how long ago did this happen?"

"I ... I don't know." He let go of the dashboard and looked at his watch. "Shit."

"What?"

"I remember checking my watch... just before they attacked us... fifteen minutes ago." He slammed his fist down on the dashboard. "Fuck!"

Will glanced at him, then back at the road. They rounded a bend, the SUV leaning precariously and the tires protesting, then he slammed on the brakes as they reached a T junction.

"Which way?"

John shook his head, leaning forward even further and looking left and right. "I don't... I don't fucking know."

Will looked left, right, then left again. He edged the vehicle forward, turned the steering wheel to the left, then hesitated. Exhaling loudly, he turned to look at John.

"John," he spoke softly.

John didn't answer, his head swiveling back and forth, the knuckles of his hands turning white as he gripped the dashboard.

"John," Will spoke louder.

"What are you waiting for?" John cried out in frustration.

"John, listen to me. We don't know which way they went, and they must be miles away by now. We'll never find them like this."

John rounded on his friend and snarled, "So we should give up? Let me drive!"

Will took his hands off the wheel and held them up. "John, think about it. They've got a fifteen minute head start, we don't know which way they've gone…." He did a quick calculation. "Even at thirty miles an hour, they will be seven to eight miles away by now, and I'm sure they'll be going faster than that, even on these narrow roads."

John knew Will was right, but he didn't want to admit it. Not just yet. He clenched his fists, adrenaline still coursing through his system. "Fuck, fuck, fuck." He punched the dashboard in frustration.

"I'm not suggesting we give up, don't get me wrong… but let's go back and speak to the police."

"The police! They're bloody useless."

Will shrugged. "But, John, what else do we do? We could roam the countryside for hours." He reached over and placed a hand on John's arm, and John flinched at the contact.

"Look mate, they've got cameras, more manpower than us. They can do a better job than the two of us alone."

John felt all the life flow out of him, and he slumped back in his seat. He took a deep breath, grimaced at the pain in his ribs, then exhaled. He gave Will a nod.

Will studied him for several moments, then put the car in gear, pulled a u-turn and headed back the way they had come.

John ground his teeth, not seeing the scenery, his eyes filling with tears of frustration.

Why, why, why?

Why Adriana? Why not him?

13

Sergeant Ethan Manners frowned at his notebook and looked up. "So you didn't see their faces, and you didn't get the registration of the van?"

He could see the muscles in the man's jaw moving as he ground his teeth together. Manners held his spare hand up in a placatory gesture. "It's okay. I understand your frustration. It must have happened so quickly. But I'm sure you understand. I have to ask these questions."

"While you're asking these questions, they're getting away!" the man growled at him.

There was something familiar about him. Manners wasn't sure what, but he felt like he had seen him before. Manners glanced down at his notebook again and read the man's name. John. John Hayes. Even the name was familiar. Then it dawned on him... when and where they had met before.

Looking up, he said, "we've met before, Mr. Hayes. The fire... your parents' house. About six or seven months ago."

John Hayes nodded but said nothing. He was clenching

and unclenching his fingers and constantly moving, shifting his weight from one foot to the other, as if he couldn't wait to get away.

The last time Manners had seen John Hayes like this was just before he grabbed a handful of his uniform and thrust him up against a fire engine, furious about a perceived lack of action.

Manners took a precautionary step backwards. "Mr. Hayes, we've issued a BOLO for a white transit van... we'll be checking them all, but I'm sure you're aware, there are thousands of them, and without a license plate number the ANPR... um... the Automatic Number Plate Recognition System won't pick it up."

John Hayes stared back at him, the muscles in his jaw still working. Although he didn't avert his eyes, Manners could tell that Hayes wasn't really focused on him; his thoughts seemed to be elsewhere.

"We'll check the traffic cameras..." He sighed. "But again, we're in a rural area. There aren't many cameras around." He paused and looked around. His constable was interviewing the man with the Pajero and behind John Hayes, two paramedics hovered by the open doors of an idling ambulance. Mr. Hayes had resisted attempts by the paramedics to check him out, pushing them away and, at one point, shouting at them to leave him alone.

"Is there anything else you think might help us? She's a journalist, right? Any enemies..." he looked down at his notes again, "that ah Adriana D'Silva might have?"

John Hayes narrowed his eyes and shook his head.

"Nothing at all? No-one you can think of?"

"No."

Manners exhaled, nodded, and closed his notebook. He

reached into his pocket and pulled out a card. "Here's my number. If you think of anything, remember anything that might help us. Just call me."

John Hayes took the card and slid it into his pocket without looking at it.

"Mr. Hayes, don't worry. We'll find her."

Again, John Hayes said nothing, just stared at him with an intensity that was unnerving.

"Um... okay." Manners looked around and caught his colleague's eye. He received a nod in reply and turned back to John. "We'll go back to the station. I'll let you know as soon as we get some news."

John Hayes nodded.

"Do you need a lift anywhere?"

He shook his head.

"Okay...You should get that wound looked at while the paramedics are here."

John turned and looked at the ambulance, but still didn't speak.

"Okay then..."

Manners turned and walked back to the patrol car. He climbed into the passenger seat and looked through the windshield at John Hayes, who was standing with his hands on his hips, staring back, as if waiting for him to leave.

Why would someone kidnap the woman? It wasn't random. It couldn't be. It had all the signs of a well-organised operation. But why?

Constable Withers opened the door and climbed behind the wheel. "Shall we go?"

"Yeah," Manners replied. His mind ran back to the last time he had met John Hayes. When he had accused his neighbor of setting fire to his parents' house. Not long afterward, there was a shootout at the Atwell Estate, and the owner disappeared, never to be seen again. There had been nothing to link Hayes to the events, but it was all a strange coincidence. And in Manners' experience, things were rarely a coincidence.

14

John waited until the patrol car rounded the bend and disappeared from sight before turning to Will.

"Asian."

"What?" Will gave him a puzzled look, glanced over at Paul and then back at John.

"They were Asian," John explained, reaching for his phone. "I saw their eyes... Through the balaclava." He dialed a Dubai number from memory and held the phone to his ear. "Get rid of them," he said with a jerk of his head toward the paramedics. "I don't need them."

Will looked like he was about to protest, then seeing John's expression, changed his mind and went off to talk to the paramedics while John waited for the phone call to be answered.

"John, how are you?"

"Ramesh, we don't have much time. Adriana's been kidnapped."

"What? When? Where?"

"I'm in England. I'll send you the location. Search for a

white Ford Transit Van in the vicinity within the last thirty minutes. Is that possible?"

John could hear the rapid movement of fingers on a computer keyboard.

"I'm starting now. Send me the location as soon as possible. Anything else I should know?"

"They were Asian, Ramesh. Three men. Professional." John grimaced and pinched the bridge of his nose with his spare hand. "I'm guessing they were Chinese."

"Shit.... You don't think....?"

"I don't know, Ramesh. Just find her."

John ended the call without waiting for an answer, then shared his location with Ramesh before slipping the phone back into his pocket.

He watched the paramedics close the ambulance doors, then climb in and pull away.

An hour ago, life had seemed perfect. He had been happy, content... now, as had happened to him so many times before, someone had ripped out his heart. Why? Did the Universe not want him to be happy?

"John?"

Will's voice dragged him back out of his hole of pity.

"Yeah?"

"Come, I'll take you home."

John stared at his friend. He didn't want to go home. He wanted to find Adriana. He couldn't sit around waiting and besides, he'd have to tell his parents, and he wasn't looking forward to that.

"They were Chinese, Will. I'm sure of it."

Will's frown deepened. "Chinese? Are you sure?"

"I'm sure."

"But why?"

John thought back to the Chinese cat he'd seen in his building lobby. He should have listened to his gut.

"Revenge, Will. Revenge."

"Shit." Will exhaled loudly and shook his head. "I thought all that was over."

John pursed his lips and frowned at the ground. "Yeah, well, it looks like it bloody well isn't."

"You should tell the police, John."

John looked up at his friend. "Tell them what?" he scoffed. "That I raided the Atwell Estate with a group of heavily armed African mercenaries and had the Chinese owner renditioned by helicopter to an unknown destination, never to be seen again. And now they've come back to get revenge?"

"Well... when you put it like that." Will made a face, unable to think of what to say next.

"This is all my fault, Will. If I had left things alone, she'd still be here."

"John, don't blame yourself. Xie was terrorizing your parents. You stood up to him, protected your parents... it was the right thing to do. I would have done the same if I'd had the balls. "

"Was it the right thing to do? Now they've taken Adriana."

"You could never have known they would do that, John."

John scowled, pulled out his phone again, and pressed redial. It was answered almost immediately.

"Anything?" he asked.

"I'm good, but not that good, John. Give me some time."

"The more time you take, the further away they get, Ramesh."

John heard a sigh above the sound of a clicking keyboard. "I know, John, I'm doing everything... one sec..."

John closed his eyes and concentrated on the sounds coming down the phone. The clicking of a keyboard, muttered words, the background hum of cooling fans.

"I'm in the ANPR. I'm checking cameras in the area. It'll take time, John, but I'll find her. There's a lot of police chatter too. They've put out a BOLO, but they've not found anything yet."

"Keep me posted, Ramesh."

John ended the call and his fingers tightened, the frustration and anger he was trying to keep a lid on threatening to crush the phone. He took a deep breath and willed himself to keep calm. Panic and self pity would not bring Adriana back. He had to keep a control on his emotions, and not let panic and grief take control. He could fix this. He had to.

He took a deep breath, ignoring the pain from his bruised ribs, and consciously made himself stand more erect, rolling his shoulders back.

Will was watching him curiously, his brow furrowed, but not saying anything.

John nodded at him. "I'm going to find her, and when I do, the people who took her will wish they had never been born."

Will nodded and reached out with his right hand and gripped his shoulder. "I'm here for you, John. Let me know what I can do."

"Thank you, Will."

"Let's get you home first." Will flicked his gaze to the side of John's head. "Let's get that cleaned up."

John followed him to the Pajero and climbed in. First things first. Find that van.

The police were looking, but his bet was on Ramesh finding it first.

15

John winced as his mother dabbed at the cut on his head.

"Sorry, dear."

John grunted, his mind elsewhere. He thought back to the kidnapping, playing the events over in his mind, slowing it down, looking for anything he may have forgotten.

The van looked like any other, nothing to distinguish it from the thousands of others on the road.

There were three men. The driver and two men in the back. All masked and dressed in black, on the shorter side of average height, slightly built, but strong. The man who seized Adriana had picked her up with ease. He remembered him sticking something in her thigh. A sedative. The man had shouted at John's attacker... but not in English.

He remembered the eyes of his assailant. Dark... narrow... Asian for sure. His gut told him they were Chinese, but how could he be certain?

He narrowed his eyes, searching his memory again. His mum was saying something to him, but he ignored her, ignored the sting of the iodine on his wound, ignored the constant throbbing in his skull, and the dull ache in his back and ribs. Something had convinced him they were Chinese. What was it?

The man had shouted twice. What had he said? John closed his eyes, narrowing his focus to a pinpoint, trying to hear the sound again. *Lee...lee* something.

"John?"

"Shhh," he shook his head irritably and renewed his focus. *Likai ta!* That was it. It sounded like Mandarin. John had spent long enough in Hong Kong to recognize both Cantonese and Mandarin. *Likai ta!*

He opened his eyes and forced an apologetic smile. "Sorry, Mum." He took her hand and moved it away from his head. "It's ok. That's enough. Thank you."

She looked surprised and opened her mouth to protest, but he cut her off with, "Where's my phone?"

He saw it on the kitchen table and picked it up. Thumbing open the browser, he searched for Google Translate and selected Simplified Chinese as a language. He wasn't sure if typing in romanised characters would work, but it was worth a try. He typed in *likai ta* and the app instantly translated it into English. *Leave him.*

He inhaled deeply and nodded to himself. His hunch had been correct.

"What is it, John?" David Hayes spoke from the other side of the kitchen table where he had been watching Carole dress John's head wound.

"One sec." John closed his eyes again and concentrated. They had said something else.... What was it?

"Xian zai."

"Sorry?"

John ignored his father and typed the words into Google Translate. *Now!*

Likai ta! Xian zai! Leave him! Now!

Chinese. Mainland Chinese, not Hong Kong Chinese.

John jumped up and began pacing the kitchen. It had to be something to do with Xie. Had to be. There was no other reason.

"John, tell us what's happening. Remember, we decided long ago, no more secrets."

John tuned back into the room and stared at his parents, who suddenly looked very old and frail, as if they had aged ten years overnight. They loved Adriana like a daughter.

He nodded and then gestured to the chair he had occupied until moments ago. "Mum, sit down. I'll tell you what I know so far."

His mum moved to the empty chair, sat down and folded the cloth she had been cleaning his wound with, placing it neatly on the table beside her.

John moved back and leaned his butt against the kitchen bench-top. He crossed his arms, looked down at the kitchen floor, then unfolded them and rested his hands on the bench-top on either side of him and looked up.

"I think Xie's people have taken her."

There was a sharp intake of breath from the table, and his parents exchanged worried glances.

"How..."

John held up his hand, interrupting his father.

"I'll explain." He took a breath. "The men's build, the shape of their eyes... it led me to believe they were Asian. I had a hunch they could be Chinese, but just now I remembered what they had shouted at each other. It was Mandarin." John saw his father's frown deepen. "There are many Chinese languages but Mandarin is the main one. It's what they speak in China. What Xie speaks... spoke."

"But... I thought that was over? That you had..." his mum trailed off, her mouth opening and closing but no sound coming out.

John shrugged, glanced at his dad, then moved over to the table, knelt down and took her hand in his. He held her eye and said, "Whatever's happening, I'll deal with it, Mum. Don't worry."

"But Adriana... why her?"

John took a deep breath then, still holding his mother's hand, turned to answer his father. "I don't know. I've been thinking about it. They could have done anything to me, but they didn't. They left me behind."

"They need you to do something."

The comment took John by surprise. Not so much what was said... because he had come to the same conclusion. No, he was more surprised by who said it. He turned to look back at his mum and nodded. "I think you're right, Mum. They're using her as a bargaining chip."

"So, what do we do now?"

John smiled at the use of 'we'. He looked at his mum, then his dad. "*We*," he emphasized the word, "have to wait and see. If we're right, I'm sure they'll get in touch."

John's phone vibrated on the table with an incoming call. As he reached for it, his father asked, "And if we aren't?"

"I don't want to think about that."

16

"Ramesh," John barked into the phone as he let go of his mother's hand and stood up.

"They've found the van. The cops."

"Where?" John asked as he paced around the kitchen.

"In a field about ten kilometers from you. I've sent you the location. Check your phone."

John put the phone on speaker, then checked his messages. Ramesh's voice squawked from the phone speaker, "The van's been torched, John."

"Shit." John cursed, then, realising what he'd said, cast a guilty glance at his parents before zooming into the map. "Why would they leave it there?"

"I'm guessing they switched cars, John. They'd know the police are looking for a white van, so they switched."

"So now we've no idea what they're driving! For fuck's sake!" John cursed, forgetting about his parents in the room. "Arrgh!" John roared. "And the police have no idea?"

"No. I've been monitoring the police channels, but they've no leads."

"Dammit!" John cursed again while clenching his right

hand into a fist and shaking it in frustration. "Dammit," he repeated.

"John wait..."

"What?"

"They don't have any leads, but I think I do."

John stopped his pacing and paused in the middle of the kitchen, his eyes locking with his mother's. "What do you mean?"

"Well, I looked around nearby and there's an airstrip. Popham Airfield."

"Popham Airfield?" John repeated and looked at his dad, who nodded. He looked back at his phone and moved the map around with his finger. "Yeah, I see it."

"I checked for any flights in the last hour."

"And?" John frowned at the phone.

"The only flight today took off forty-five minutes ago. Tail number Golf Alpha Foxtrot Delta Five. A Cessna 206 Stationair owned by Delta Aviation Ltd. The company is based in Jersey and my guess is it's a shell corporation.... I've not had time to dig deeper."

"Hmmm, any cameras there?"

"They've got a couple of webcams, but the coverage is mainly of the runway. I'm not able to see who boarded the plane, but get this... they filed a flight plan for an airstrip in Portugal."

"You're kidding?"

"No. One sec..."

John heard rapid typing, then Ramesh spoke again. "Aerodromo de Torres Vedra."

John shook his head. "Never heard of it."

"It's about forty-five kilometers from Lisbon."

John screwed up his face and scratched his head while he thought. "It's too much of a coincidence."

"That's what I thought. I'll dig deeper and see what I can find out."

"Thanks." John exhaled loudly. "Dad, how far away is this Popham Airfield?"

David Hayes was tapping away on his phone and looked up at John's question. "About twenty-five minutes, son."

John nodded and returned his attention to the call. "Ramesh, find out what you can. I'm heading to the airfield to see if I can find anyone who saw the plane takeoff and who was on it."

"I'm on it."

The call ended, and John looked up at his parents. His mum stared at the table, her bottom lip between her teeth, but his dad was still tapping away on his phone. Before John could say anything, his dad spoke up, "He said forty-five minutes ago, right?"

"Yes, why?"

David Hayes looked up. "A Cessna 206 has a cruising speed of around one hundred and fifty knots, and the distance between the two airfields is about eight hundred and fifty nautical miles. I calculate a flight time of around five and a half to six hours depending on the weather. If they took off forty-five minutes ago, then they'll land in four and a half hours at the earliest."

John blinked in surprise, exchanged a quick glance with his mum, then checked the time on his watch. "Okay. I need to get moving." He typed a quick message to Ramesh with the estimated arrival time and then moved toward the door.

"I'm coming with you." John's father was already standing.

John began to protest, but his father stopped him with a raised hand. "Don't argue."

John held his stare, then shrugged. "Suit yourself."

17

John completed the twenty-five minute journey in twenty, pushing the Porsche to its limits.

His father sat silently beside him, not even protesting at the speeds John was taking. The only sign of discomfort was when his left leg moved as if to apply the brakes when John entered a corner at twice the recommended speed.

John spotted the entrance and braked hard, heel and toeing as he downshifted, then turned in, applying a swift application of opposite lock as the back of the car stepped out, narrowly avoiding swiping the gatepost as he drove through. He raced down the driveway, ignoring the speed limit signs, then braked, looking for an office, when his father spoke for the first time since they left the house.

"Over there."

John followed his directions and pulled up outside a green corrugated iron aircraft hangar.

"I'll do the talking," David said gruffly and was out of the car with a speed belying his years. John, more than a little bewildered, turned off the engine, climbed out, and followed him toward the hangar.

Inside, two men in overalls stood beneath a World War Two era Spitfire with its engine cowling open. One of the men raised a hand in greeting, then wiped his hands on a rag and met David halfway. He smiled at him, then looked over at the Porsche and said something John couldn't make out, but set both the men laughing.

David turned, and as John approached, made the introductions.

"This is my son, John."

The elderly man held out a calloused, oil stained hand and shook John's with a firm grip. "Hi John, Harry. That's a beautiful car you've got there."

John smiled blandly, doing little to hide his impatience. There were more important things to discuss than his car, and he was still struggling to understand his father's connection with the airstrip. David gave him a look, then placed a hand on Harry's shoulder. "Harry, we need your help. It's rather urgent."

Harry arched his eyebrows and looked from David to John, then back again. "Of course. Have you got yourself in a spot of bother?"

David smiled and shook his head. "No, no, but did you see a plane take off about an hour ago? A Cessna 206?"

Harry frowned. "Yes, the Stationair. Nice little plane. Very reliable."

"Did you see who was on it?" John interjected.

"What's this about?"

"I'll explain later, Harry, but did you see who was on it? It's important."

Harry frowned deeper, then puffed out his cheeks and exhaled. "I didn't see close up, but it was a full load. Three men plus the pilot, and they had a large bag. It looked heavy. Two of them were carrying it between them."

John stepped closer and grabbed Harry by the arm. "Can you describe them? Anything that stood out."

Harry hesitated, looked at David, who nodded encouragement, then said, "Well... they were all in black..." He frowned deeper, searching his memory, "they were quite far from here... but I think they were Asian."

"Fuck," John cursed, letting go of Harry's arm and stepping away.

"What's going on?"

David looked at John, then stepped closer to Harry and lowered his voice. "They've taken something from us."

"Oh... I see. Have you told the police?"

"No... not yet."

John turned back and asked, "Have you seen them around here before?"

Harry shook his head. "No. The plane only arrived two hours ago. Refueled, and then the pilot hung around until the others turned up in that Audi over there."

John turned, spotted the Audi and was off at a sprint, pulling out his phone at the same time. He reached the dark blue Audi A6 parked in the carpark and peered inside. It was empty; the interior stripped clean. He tried the door handle, but it was locked. Walking around to the front, he dialed Ramesh. Before Ramesh could say anything, he asked, "Can you find out who owns a dark blue Audi, registration number...?" He read out the registration and could hear Ramesh typing. After a moment he added, "It was them, Ramesh. I'm at the airfield and we have a witness who spotted three Asian males with a large bag getting on that flight."

"Shit…" Ramesh kept typing, and then, "Stolen. Yesterday from Basingstoke."

"Shit." John raised a fist in frustration. He turned around and looked back toward the hangar at his father and Harry, the phone still pressed to his ear. "The bastards put her in a bag, Ramesh. They put her in a fucking bag!"

Ramesh stopped typing.

"I'm going to hunt them down, Ramesh, and when I find them, they're going to wish they had never been born."

There was a long silence, then Ramesh's voice came over the phone, determined, confident. "Anything you need, John, let me know. I'll not work on anything else until we find them."

"Thanks, Ramesh," John replied automatically, but his mind was racing. They had over an hour's head start and would land in another country. What could he do? How could he regain the upper hand?

"They'll land in five hours, Ramesh. See what you can find out and keep me posted."

"What are you going to do, John?"

"I don't know, Ramesh. Right now I have no fucking idea, but I'm not giving up without a fight. I'll get her back if it's the last thing I do."

18

"But you have to call the police."

John heard Harry urging his father as he neared the two men.

John held up his hand. "We will, we will." He scanned the aircraft parked in a row along the airstrip. "Do you have anything here that will get me to Portugal?" He turned his wrist and looked at his G-Shock. "Preferably something that will get me there in under five hours."

Harry was already shaking his head. "You'd need a jet. But they can't take off and land here. The airstrip is grass and too short."

"What's the fastest plane you've got?"

Harry frowned and rubbed the back of his head, then glanced at David as if for reassurance. David nodded.

Harry turned and ran his eye along the row of parked aircraft. "Well... there's the Piper... no, the Cessna over there."

"The 210?" David asked, and John did a double take.

"Yes, the 210. It will cruise at about 170 to 175 knots..."

David Hayes had pulled his phone out and was doing

some calculations. Looking up, he said to John, "You'll be there in around five hours, but it depends on the weather."

"Shit!" John cursed and threw his hands in the air. "Shit, shit, shit."

He continued cursing as he paced around. What should he do? What should he do? He looked again at his watch. It would be close. He chewed his lip and stared at the white Cessna. But at least he would be in the same country.

He spun around. "I need someone to fly me in that plane to Portugal immediately."

Harry paled and his jaw went slack. "But...but..."

"I'll pay whatever it costs."

"But it's not my plane."

"Who owns it?"

"Well... Devon Maxwell."

"Do you have his number? Call him. Tell him I'll rent it for whatever he asks." John paused.... "Can you fly it?"

"Ahh... yes I can but..."

"I'll pay you for your time, whatever you want, but we have to go now."

Harry just stared at him, his mouth hanging open.

David placed a hand on his arm and spoke gently. "He's good for it, Harry. I'll vouch for him."

Harry hesitated, still not saying anything.

David added, "They've kidnapped his girlfriend, Harry. She was in that bag."

His eyes widened, and he gulped, but the words had the desired effect. "I'll do it. But I need to fuel the plane and run some checks."

"How long will that take?"

"Half an hour."

John grimaced, but there was nothing he could do. "Okay, as quick as you can, please."

Harry nodded. "And you'll need your passport."

"Oh shit, yes. Bugger." He turned to his father, "Come on, Dad, I have to go home and get it."

"I'll stay here, son, with Harry. In case he needs help."

John nodded and sprinted to his car.

19

"What's going on, David?"

Harry had just spent five-minutes on the phone convincing the owner they weren't doing anything illegal and assuring him he would be compensated for the use of his plane.

David Hayes paused beneath the wing of the Cessna and gazed up at the flaps, thinking about what to say. Harry was a good friend. They had a shared interest in building model planes, and David had spent many an hour at the airstrip watching Harry work on the Spitfire. But even with a friend, there was only so much he could share. He took a breath. The best lies were based on some element of truth, so he did the best he could. "Adriana, the lady who's been kidnapped... she's a journalist."

Harry nodded slowly, as if he was starting to understand.

Encouraged, David continued, "She specializes in stories about corruption and criminality in business. She's won awards for it."

"So she's upset someone with an article and they've kidnapped her?"

David shrugged and looked back up at the wing, hoping his face wasn't giving anything away. "Something like that," he muttered.

"So... why doesn't your son...?"

"John."

"Yes, John. Why doesn't he leave it to the police? We know the flight, we have the flight plan. He can let the police know and they'll apprehend them when they land."

David nodded. "He'll do that," he assured him, even though he wasn't sure if that was John's plan at all. "But my son... he's a man of action. He won't be content to stand by and leave things up to others. Besides, he'll want to be there for Adriana when the police rescue her."

"Well, my friend, I'll do my best to make sure he's there as soon as I can."

David smiled with his mouth, but not his eyes. "I appreciate it, Harry, I really do. I'll buy you a pint when this is all over."

20

John slammed the heel of his palm on the horn then swerved to overtake a slower moving car, the right hand wheels of the Porsche dropping off the road and into the dirt, struggling for grip as he pushed the sports car through the gap between the car and the hedgerow.

He ignored the honking from the car he'd passed, applied a little corrective lock on the steering wheel as the car fish-tailed, then when all four wheels were back on the tarmac, planted his foot on the accelerator and sped on.

"Don't kill yourself, John," said a voice in his earbuds.

"I can't waste time, Ramesh. I'm still going to be at least half an hour behind them." John shouted to make himself heard above the roar of the engine.

"I know. I know. Is there anyone there who can help you?"

"No-one, Ramesh, it's down to me."

"Will you inform the police?"

John made a face, while braking heavily for a corner. He downshifted, aimed for the apex, then accelerated out of the bend, climbing through the gears, allowing the car to run wide on the exit, using all the road.

"Would *you* involve the police?" John shot back, knowing full well Ramesh shared the same opinion of the authorities.

There was a heavy silence, and John concentrated on the road.

"Maybe in this case you should," Ramesh replied after a while. "They can intercept the plane. At least see who's on it. Maybe even search it?"

John thought about it as he overtook two cars in a row, then braked hard as a stop sign loomed ahead. He didn't stop, slowing just enough to make the turn, then accelerated away again. John had a distrust of the authorities born from experience. But maybe this time Ramesh was right? Maybe the police were the best option.

"Okay, I'll call them, but I'm not leaving everything up to them. So see what you can do, cameras, police chatter, anything. I don't believe it will be as easy as the police picking them up at the airport. If it's the Chinese, they'll have some tricks up their sleeves."

"I'm on it."

"Keep me posted, Ramesh."

John ended the call and braked for the entrance to the farm. He really didn't want to get the police involved, but it was unlikely he would reach Portugal in time, and if there was anything that could help, he had to try it.

He pulled up with a screech of tires outside his parents' cottage and, leaving the engine running, jumped out and ran to the front door.

Inside, he dashed upstairs to his room, retrieved his passport, and then paused for a moment to see if there was anything else he might need. But he had everything with him. Wallet, passport, and phone.

He descended two stairs at a time, almost colliding with his mother at the foot of the stairs.

"Sorry, Mum. I've got to go. Dad will explain." He gave her a quick hug, kissed her on the top of the head, and ran for the door.

"John, what's going on?" she called after him.

"I've found out where they've taken her," he shouted over his shoulder. Running to the car, he climbed in as his mum appeared in the doorway.

"Where, John?"

"Portugal," he called out, pulled the door closed, slammed the car in reverse and reversed out of the driveway at high speed. As he selected first gear and pulled away, he tried to forget the look on his mum's face.

21

John dialed with one hand, then dropped the phone in his lap as the call rang out and he concentrated on the road.

"Sergeant Manners."

"This is John Hayes, Sergeant. I know where they've taken her. I need you to contact the Portuguese police."

There was silence in John's ear, and he could feel a fiery ball of anger expanding in the pit of his stomach. He pressed harder on the accelerator; the car flying along the narrow country lanes. He swerved around a car, narrowly missing one coming in the other direction, setting off a cacophony of angry honking.

"Where are you, Mr. Hayes?"

"It doesn't matter where I am. Didn't you hear what I just said?"

"Mr. Hayes, please lower your voice and start from the beginning."

"Oh, for fuck's sake," John cursed. "A witness saw them boarding a plane at Popham Airfield."

"Saw who?" Manners interrupted.

"Three Chinese men dressed in black and carrying a large bag. They took off an hour ago, headed for an airstrip in Portugal. Call the Portuguese police and get them to meet the plane."

There was silence again, and John shook his head. He knew it was a waste of time.

"Three Chinese men?"

"Yes. They were Chinese. I saw their eyes and heard them speak."

"You didn't tell me that, Mr. Hayes."

"Well, I'm telling you now, for fuck's sake."

There was silence again, then, "How could you possibly know these are the same people? And how did you get this information?"

"Will you please stop asking stupid fucking questions?"

"Mr. Hayes, I know you're upset, but there's no need to be rude. I want to help you, but please understand I can't go to a foreign nation's police without evidence."

"Argh!" John ground his teeth together. "Look, it doesn't matter how I found out. Three men dressed in black turned up at Popham Airfield in a stolen Audi. They boarded a flight for Portugal and loaded a large, heavy bag. It's them, I'm telling you."

John could hear Manners sigh even over the sound of the racing engine and his grip on the steering wheel tightened with frustration.

"Look, I'll have someone send you the tail number, the flight plan, and the estimated arrival time. Do whatever you can, just get the police to meet the flight. Trust me, Sergeant, these are the kidnappers. It'll be on your conscience if you sit on your arse and do nothing." John realized he was being harsh, but he was so filled with adrenaline and frustration that he no longer cared.

"Okay," Manners sighed. "I can't promise anything, but I'll see what I can do."

"Thank you. You won't regret it."

"I hope not Mr. Hayes. I hope not." Manners paused. "And what are you planning to do?"

"I'm going after them." John heard Manners protest and ended the call.

It took another ten minutes to reach the airfield. He ignored the five missed calls from Manners and drove the Porsche onto the apron, sliding to a stop beside the waiting Cessna. He jumped out and tossed the keys to his dad. "Look after her, Dad. I'll call when I land."

His dad pocketed the keys, then stepped forward and gripped John by the shoulders. "Good luck, son. Bring her back to us."

"I will, Dad." Before David could see any doubt in John's face, he turned and headed toward the aircraft. "Let's go, Harry, we've no time to waste."

22

It was the noise she noticed first, a steady drone vibrating through her skull. She fought back the urge to vomit as a wave of nausea swept over her. Her temples throbbed, and she had lost the feeling in her arms. Everything was dark. Thin spots of light ran in a line just above her face and when she moved her head, it rubbed against some sort of heavy, coarse material.

What happened to her? Where was she?

She searched through the fog of drowsiness and nausea, struggling to work out what had happened. She tried to change position. There was a hard surface under her right side and her legs were bent back behind her. She attempted to stretch out her legs and roll over, but the coarse material restricted her movements and she could not move her arms. Her breath quickened, and she opened her mouth to cry out, and that was when her befuddled senses realized she had been gagged. The panic increased, and she struggled to move again.

"Help!" she cried out, but with the gag, it was barely audible above the constant drone.

Her eyelids drooped and her breathing slowed and deepened as she fell unconscious again.

It was a sudden churn of her stomach followed by a momentary feeling of weightlessness, then pain shooting through her as her body hit a hard surface that woke her. She retched against the gag, then swallowed the contents of her stomach back down. The background drone was still there, but now it rose and fell, and the surface she was lying on moved up and down. In a flash, she realized she must be on a plane, although she still could not see anything. Again she tried to move, to get some feeling into her limbs, but she only increased the throbbing in her head and the urge to vomit.

Fighting the situation wasn't helping, so she lay back and closed her eyes, slowed her breathing down and concentrated on her surroundings. She was on a plane, of that she was sure, but it sounded like a small aircraft. Something was wrapped around her, which accounted for the darkness, but it was light outside because she could still see the line of light above her.

Why?

Then she remembered. Walking with John... the van... the men in black... the sharp pain in her leg.

After that, it wasn't so clear. She remembered someone picking her up and dropping her in the van. But the last thing she remembered was seeing John lying on the side of the road as the door of the van slid shut.

A tear rolled from the corner of her eye and down her cheek. Was John okay? Was he alive? Who had done this?

Then Adriana got angry. Now was not the time to feel sorry for herself. She was alive, and there must be a reason. She would wait and see what happened. There had to be a way out, and she had to believe John was okay. She had seen what he was capable of, and woe betide anyone who thought they could cross him.

23

The flight had seemed endless. John was on the right-hand side of the tiny cockpit and, in normal circumstances, would have enjoyed the experience. But all he could think about was Adriana drugged and stuffed in a bag. His feelings fluctuated between despair and anger and he worked on fueling the anger. Anger would get him further than feeling sorry for himself or Adriana.

The old guy, Harry, had attempted to engage John in conversation, but John discouraged him with monosyllabic answers and then closed his eyes, hoping Harry would take the hint.

It had worked, and he remained silent for the rest of the flight, only speaking when they were in sight of the Portuguese coastline.

John used the time to think.

What did he know?

The men were Chinese, and they had taken Adriana alive. Drugged her and carried her off, leaving him alive too. It was quick and professional, and given that they were now flying to Portugal, suggested a large organisation, if not a state actor.

So that led to the next question.

Why?

It had to be something to do with Xie. There was no other connection with China. But Xie had been missing for months. So why now?

Adriana's articles had stirred up some international interest, but that had long since died down, replaced by the next scandal in the news cycle.

If it was revenge, then why didn't they kill them both? Something they could have done at anytime in the last seven months.

They had wanted them both alive. Why?

Below him, the North Atlantic Ocean stretched out as far as he could see to his right as they followed the coastline south. He heard Harry's voice in the headphones as he spoke to Portuguese Air Traffic Control, then felt a hand on his arm. Looking over, he saw Harry pointing through the windscreen. Ahead, still some distance away but visible through the wispy cloud, John could see at a forty-five degree angle to the coast a long straight patch of sun burnt ground with a strip of concrete running alongside it. "Is that it?"

"It is. We'll be on the ground before you know it."

John glanced at his watch. They had made good time, Harry coaxing as much speed as he could from the plane. But he estimated they would still land after the Chinese. John straightened up in his seat and tightened the straps of his four-point harness. Adrenaline surged through his system and he willed himself to stay calm while straining to make out detail on the airstrip ahead of them.

As they descended, the plane pitched and yawed, and

John's stomach lurched into his throat as they hit a large air pocket. The movement thrust him against the straps of his harness sending a new wave of pain through his battered body. Forcing himself to ignore it, he watched Harry make adjustments with the yoke and the rudder pedals, but the old pilot didn't seem the least bit bothered by the turbulence.

John returned his attention back to the airfield. He could now make out the hangars at the top end of the runway, and several planes parked on the apron as they descended lower over the sea. The white caps of the waves were now clearly visible, and then they crossed the golden sand of the *Praia de Fisica*. Red-tiled roofs of the town rushed up to meet them and John twisted sideways in his seat, looking over Harry's shoulder as they passed the hangars and parked aircraft.

There was no sign of the police anywhere.

Harry touched down with only the slightest of bumps, then reduced the engine speed and applied the brakes, forcing John forward against the straps of his harness.

John ignored the instructions from the air traffic controller in his headset, impatient to get out of the plane, as his phone connected to the local network and began buzzing with incoming messages. Messages from Ramesh, his dad, Sergeant Manners, and an unknown number.

He tapped on Ramesh's message first. *Call me.*

John pulled off his headset and dialed his number as Harry turned the plane and headed back down the runway toward the hangars.

It was only a moment before the phone call connected.

"They got away, John."

John's heart sank into his stomach.

24

"How?" John couldn't believe what he was hearing. He tugged at his shoulder straps loosening the harness, and leaned forward, peering through the windscreen.

Harry pointed at a plane that looked very much like their own. "That's the one."

John's eyes scanned the tail number for confirmation. *Golf Alpha Foxtrot Delta Five.*

But there was no-one around. No passengers. No pilot. No police.

Acid bile filled the back of his throat. He had known he might be late, but had hoped the police might do something.

"What happened, Ramesh? Did the cops not come through?"

"The Brits did their bit, John. That wasn't the problem."

"Then what the fuck happened?"

"I don't know. I hacked into the airfield cameras and saw the plane arrive. There was a police car waiting for them. I saw a man get out of the plane and talk to the police and then, after about five minutes, the police got back into their car and drove off."

"What?" John screwed up his face and made a fist with his left hand, wanting to thump something but finding nothing in the small cockpit for him to unleash his frustration on.

"Yeah. Then they all piled into a dark blue van and drove off."

"The bag. Did you see the bag?"

"I did. They loaded it into the van before leaving. It took two of them to carry it."

"Bastards!" John cursed. "And then? Did you see where they went?"

"Sorry, John. They went out the gate and turned left. That's all I know."

"Fuck!" John cursed again. "Shit. I'll call you back."

He ended the call and stared out at the plane they had chased from England.

Harry had been silent, busy parking the Cessna and powering down the engine. But now he turned and looked at John. "What do you want me to do?"

John didn't answer. He just stared out at the Stationair, wondering what the hell he could do next.

"John?"

John snapped out of it and looked at Harry. "They got away, Harry. They got away."

"I heard... I'm sorry. I really am."

The two sat staring at the aircraft, neither of them saying anything. After a long pause, Harry asked, "Do you want me to fly you somewhere else? I'll need to refuel, but I'll take you anywhere."

John nodded slowly, deep in thought, then shook his head. "No... thank you, Harry. I'm getting out here." He turned and held out his hand. "Thank you for flying me here. Let me know how much I owe you. I'll transfer it as soon as I get time."

"Don't worry, John. No rush. Your dad said you're good for it." He paused. "Look, I'm going to find a room. I'll stay the night. At my age, I don't want to fly another four hours without getting some rest. So I'll be here until tomorrow." He took a deep breath. "What I'm trying to say is, I'll still be here if you need me."

John nodded slowly, then smiled. "Thank you, Harry. I appreciate that. And add the room onto my bill."

Harry studied John's face for a long time before replying. "I hope you find her, John."

"So do I, Harry, so do I."

25

Sergeant Ethan Manners tapped a nervous rhythm on his desk with his index finger, while staring blindly at the open folder in front of him. He had just come off the phone with his counterparts in Portugal and was deeply disturbed.

There was much more to Adriana D'Silva's kidnapping than met the eye. And now when he thought about it, there was much more to John Hayes than met the eye.

The odds of the man who accused his Chinese neighbor of burning down his parents' house also alleging his partner was kidnapped by unidentified Asian men and taken to another country seemed highly improbable. His frown deepened as he stopped tapping and leaned back in his chair, rubbing his face with both hands. The neighbor's sudden disappearance shortly after the fire, under suspicious circumstances, only added to the confusion. What on earth was happening?

He had a strong feeling this case was well above his pay grade. What at first seemed like a local kidnapping was now an international matter, possibly involving foreign governments. Common sense told him he should pass the investigation up the food chain, hand it on to someone way more senior.

What was the name of that guy who paid him a visit when the Chinese neighbor disappeared? The posh government guy from London who was obviously a spook, even though he claimed to work for the Ministry of Foreign Affairs? He had a double-barrelled name. Chumley something. Perhaps he should call him? Tell him about his suspicions. He had left a card. It must still be around somewhere.

Before he could decide, his phone rang, and he picked it up absentmindedly.

"Sergeant Manners."

"What the hell happened?"

He recognized the voice instantly, and he glanced up at the clock on his wall. John Hayes. He must have just landed.

"I'm assuming you've reached the…" he opened the file and looked down at his notes. "Aerodromo de Torres Vedras."

"Why didn't the cops stop them?"

Manners could hear the frustration in his voice. "They couldn't, Mr. Hayes. The passengers were traveling on diplomatic passports. Chinese diplomatic passports."

There was no sound from the other end of the line.

Manners sat forward and leaned his elbows on his desk. "What's really going on, Mr. Hayes? I get the feeling you're not telling me everything."

"Tell me everything they said," John Hayes replied, ignoring the question. "What did the cops tell you?"

Manners made a face and took a breath. "They just said the passengers were four Asian men with Chinese diplomatic passports. Another Chinese national met them in a vehicle with consular plates."

"What about the bag? Why didn't they check the bag?" John's volume was rising.

"They're not allowed to, Mr. Hayes. There are certain procedures. We don't have evidence of criminality, just a... hunch of yours," Manners sighed. "And there's even less we can do when the people involved are diplomats."

"So you let them get away."

Manners winced at the accusation. "Mr. Hayes, I did what you asked. I called in significant favors to get the Portuguese police to meet the aircraft. With no concrete evidence. There's nothing more I can do."

He thought he heard John Hayes swear, but wasn't sure.

"I assure you, Mr. Hayes, we're doing everything we can here in Winchester to track down Ms. D'Silva. But we can't go running after every hunch or rumor without something to back it up."

"Don't worry, I'll handle it from here."

Manners' eyebrows shot up. What? Who did this guy think he was? "I'm sorry. What did you say?"

"Did you at least get the plate number for the blue van?"

Manners frowned again. Had he mentioned the color of the van? Perhaps he had. He stared at the sheet of handwritten notes in front of him. Should he share the information with Mr. Hayes? Protocol said no.

"Come on, you have that information."

It couldn't harm. It was another country, and he doubted Mr. Hayes could do anything with the information. "Charlie November, Two Three Alpha Bravo," he recited down the phone. He heard Hayes repeat the information, then asked, "Why would the Chinese government be involved in kidnapping Ms. D'Silva? If that's who did it?"

It was only after a long silence that he realized John Hayes had hung up.

26

John texted the registration number of the van to Ramesh, then walked over to the administration building. He pushed open the door and entered an office with three desks and pictures of light aircraft on the walls. A middle-aged woman at the nearest desk looked up from her keyboard and peered at him over the rims of the glasses perched on the end of her nose.

"*Bom dia,*" John greeted her in Portuguese.

"*Bom dia.*"

John flashed her a big smile. "I need a taxi. Can you please help me?"

She nodded, reached for her phone and, after a brief wait, had a conversation that ended in a laugh and multiple '*obrigadas.*' She hung up, her face turning serious again, and said, "Ten minutes."

"*Obrigado,*" John replied, still smiling, then turned and headed for the door. The less conversation, the better. So far, no-one had asked for his passport and he didn't want to waste time with formalities. He stepped back outside and moved away from the office window. Hopefully, if she couldn't see him, she would forget about him.

John looked back at Harry's plane. The old guy was in conversation with a man in overalls and pointing at the engine. John had still not discovered how his father knew him so well.

His father.

He must be worried sick.

John reached for his phone and was about to dial when he remembered the message from the unknown number. Switching to the messaging app, he scrolled down and tapped on it.

"Fuck!" he cursed out loud.

Xie for D'Silva.

A chill ran down his spine. In the back of his mind, he had known it was all connected, but this was confirmation.

His legs weakened as panic took over, and he leaned back against the brick wall of the administration building, no longer trusting his legs to support him.

The Chinese government had kidnapped the woman he loved, and the man they wanted in return was probably dead.

He was screwed, and so was Adriana.

John fought back waves of self pity and despair. The Chinese government? No way! He couldn't deal with this sort of thing. Who was he? He was nobody.

His phone vibrated in his hand, and his heart rate spiked sending a renewed pounding through his temples. He dared to look at the screen. An incoming call from his father. In a daze, he answered the call and held the phone to his ear.

"Son, is she okay?"

John took a deep breath and shook his head as if his

father could see him. "I failed, Dad, I failed. I got here too late."

"Oh... I'm sorry, John. W... wh... what do we do now?"

His father's voice sounded muffled, and John felt as if he had been drugged. John could hear what he was saying, but there was a disconnect between his ears and his brain.

He shook his head then reached up and grabbed a handful of hair and pulled hard, the pain in his scalp going someway to clearing his head.

"John, John... are you still there?"

"Yeah," John sighed, and pushed himself away from the wall. "I'm here." He shook his right leg out, then his left. "I don't know what to do, Dad. I don't know... I've failed. I couldn't keep her safe. She's gone."

"John!" His father snapped, the sound sending a jolt of adrenaline through his body. A memory flashed before his eyes. He was a young boy again, his father glaring down at him and shaking his finger.

"Listen to me, son. You haven't failed. You just haven't succeeded yet. You'll find her and you'll rescue her. I know you will."

"But..." John still felt like that young boy.

"No excuses, John. I know what you've done before. You're a capable and resourceful man. Look at what you did with Xie, when he was terrorizing your mother and me. Think about that. You did that. You fixed the problem. You, John. My son."

"And look what's happened now because of what I did," John protested.

"That's rubbish thinking, John. You had no idea this would happen. You protected your family. You stood up to a bully, and you dealt with him. I'm proud of you, John. I'm proud of everything you've achieved in your life, and you should be too. You can do it again."

John didn't reply. His eyes roamed the airfield... the runway... the windsock flapping in the breeze... the rows of parked aircraft... Harry and the aircraft mechanic walking toward a hangar.

His father continued, "What about the stories you told your mother and me? How you dealt with that terrible man in India...[1] the mercenaries in Oman.[2] The girl you rescued in Syria.[3] A war zone, for goodness' sake! That was you, John."

His father paused for breath. "And do you know what that makes you, son?"

"No, Dad."

"An extraordinary human being, John. You've had the balls, if you pardon my French, to stand up and fight for what's right. And you'll do it again. I know you will. Don't let this setback stop you from doing the right thing. Find Adriana and bring her back to your mother and me."

John nodded, feeling a little better.

"I'm immensely proud of you, son. Immensely proud, and I have the utmost faith in your ability to fix this."

"Thank you, Dad."

"Just take it one step at a time. What's the next thing you can do? Focus on that. And when that's done, choose the next thing."

His dad was right. Eat the elephant. One bite at a time.

He took a deep breath, rolled his shoulders back and, standing taller, he exhaled. "You're right, Dad. You're right."

"Dads are always right."

John couldn't help but chuckle. "Tell Mum I'm okay and I love her. I'll be away until this is done."

"May God protect you, son, and keep us posted."

"I will."

John set his jaw in a determined thrust, ended the call, and watched as a beige Mercedes with a taxi sign on the roof cruised through the entrance gate and rolled toward him.

He would get her back and then he would make sure that nothing like this ever happened again.

---

1. See "The Guru: John Hayes #7", and "Faith: John Hayes #8"
2. See "No Escape: John Hayes #4"
3. See "Payback: John Hayes #6"

27

She was woken by the sound of a zipper being drawn back, and then a flood of bright light forced her eyes shut again. Hands grabbed her roughly under the arms and hauled her out of what she now realized was a large bag.

They dragged her across the floor, her legs completely numb and unable to support her, and then dumped her onto a mattress.

She attempted to open her eyes again, blinking furiously against the bright light, struggling to adapt. She saw legs, black legs, perhaps two people, and she felt fingers at the back of her head untying the gag. It fell free from her mouth and she gasped, sucking in lungfuls of air. She heard a snip and her numb arms fell to the mattress as if they weren't connected to her body. She opened her eyes wider, trying to see who was in the room with her. Two figures in black walked away toward the end of the room. There was a grind of steel and a waft of air as a large full height door at the end of the room opened and the two men disappeared through it. Then the door clanged shut, leaving her alone on the mattress.

Apart from the mattress, a pillow, and a rolled-up blanket, there was nothing else in the room. The room was long but narrow and the walls weren't flat, instead broken by alternating ridges and grooves. Something about it seemed familiar. Sheets of chipped and splintered plywood covered the floor, and at the far end was a large double door which took up the entire end wall. The light came from a single source in the ceiling, a circular disc of harsh white fluorescent light.

Her extremities protested as the blood rushed back into her limbs, her fingertips and toes twitching with pins and needles. She clenched and unclenched her hands, forcing the blood to move around. Sitting upright with her legs stretched out before her, she leaned back against the wall of the room. The wall was cold, and she realized it was steel. A flash of recognition ran through her mind. She was in a shipping container.

There was the sound of steel on steel, and the door at the end opened up again. An arm tossed several plastic bottles of water inside, then slid a plate of food onto the floor before the door closed again.

Adriana contemplated calling out, but figured it would be a waste of time. She pushed herself to her feet, leaning against the wall for support as a wave of nausea washed over her. Her head still throbbed and her mouth was dry. She eyed the bottles of water and slowly, one hand against the wall for support, shuffled toward the front of the room. It was slow going, her legs filled with lead and her sense of balance upset by the drugs they had used.

She reached the front and bent down, grasping for a bottle. As she stood up, she felt dizzy again, and she leaned against the wall, her eyelids screwed shut until the dizziness passed. When she opened them, she read the label on the water bottle. It looked familiar, and it was a moment before she realized why. The red text on a white label. *Luso.* One of Portugal's most well-known brands of bottled water. Was she back in Portugal? But why? Why would someone go to the trouble of kidnapping her in England and then bring her back here? It made no sense.

She unscrewed the top and gulped down the lukewarm, plastic tasting water. With the last mouthful, she rinsed her mouth, finally feeling a little better. Her stomach rumbled, and she contemplated the plate of food on the floor. No, not plate, bowl. A bowl of noodles in soup with a pair of chopsticks. Was she hallucinating? She shook her head and peered at it again. Noodles? Chopsticks? What the hell was going on?

28

Danny Chan slowed his battered Seat Leon and eyed Yu-Ming.

"Is this it?"

Yu-Ming studied the screen of his phone and nodded. "Yes, here on the right."

Danny slowed further, then turned into the narrow entranceway beside a two-story brick warehouse building. He pulled into the parking, turned off the engine, and studied the building in his mirror. It looked like it hadn't been occupied for a long time. The paint was peeling from the window frames and weeds sprouted from cracks in the carpark's surface. If it wasn't for the dark blue van parked beside them, Danny would have assumed he was in the wrong place.

"What do you think we're doing here?"

Yu-Ming shrugged. "I don't care. As long as we're not watching that *lao wai* anymore."

Danny nodded. He also welcomed the change from sitting in an apartment watching some boring white guy go about his day. "Well, let's find out."

He climbed out, waited for Yu-Ming to get out, and then locked the door. The area looked pretty shady and even though his car was well past its prime, it was his only asset and he couldn't afford to have it stolen.

He nodded at the van. "Embassy plates."

Yu-Ming grinned and gave a thumbs up. "Cool."

Danny walked over to the wooden door beside the loading bay and tried the handle. It was locked. But someone had to be inside, otherwise the van wouldn't be there. He banged on the door with his fist, then stood back and looked up at the camera. A red light blinked at him, and a few minutes later, he heard the door unlocking, and it swung inwards.

Danny glanced back at Yu-Ming, then stepped inside. Behind the door stood a hard-looking man dressed entirely in black tactical clothing. He gave Danny a hard stare, then once Yu-Ming was inside, closed the door behind him and locked it. Without a word, he walked away across the warehouse to several trestle tables and chairs in front of a shipping container. Around the table sat three more men, all Chinese, and all dressed the same. No-one spoke.

Danny raised a hand. "Ah... hello... *Ni Hao.*"

The man who had opened the door, ignored him, sat down and began reassembling a hand gun.

Danny noticed more weapons on the table, and he froze. This wasn't what he had signed up for.

Before he could say anything, he heard Yu-Ming speaking in Mandarin. Danny struggled to understand, only catching a word here and there.

One man, older than the others, grunted and beckoned them closer.

He said something to Danny, then noticing Danny's lack

of comprehension, switched to English. "You don't speak Chinese?"

Danny shook his head.

"Why not?"

Danny looked from him to the other men, then back. "I was born here. I'm Portuguese."

A flash of irritation passed swiftly across the man's face. A younger man with a bleached mane of hair and a tattooed neck, muttered something under his breath, prompting a laugh from the other two. The older man didn't react, still staring at Danny with apparent disdain.

Once more, he spoke in Mandarin and Yu-Ming replied. Again Danny couldn't follow the conversation, but whatever was said, the man nodded and stood up. He was in his mid-forties, lean with closely cropped hair. Veins stood out on his muscled forearms, and just visible below his rolled-up sleeves was the end of a tattoo. What looked like the head of a dragon, intricately tattooed in red and blue.

"Inside that," he switched to English and jerked his head toward the shipping container. "Is a very important prisoner."

Danny turned his gaze on the shipping container, troubled thoughts racing through his mind. Watching a man in his flat was one thing, but a prisoner?

"Stay here, watch the prisoner, and wait for further instructions."

"But...?"

Ignoring him, the man pointed at a stack of plastic water bottles and cardboard boxes. "Over there is plenty of food and water." He turned back and glared at Danny. "No-one comes in or out, including you two."

Danny glanced at Yu-Ming, who had a gleam in his eye and was nodding eagerly.

The man barked an instruction in Mandarin and the other men stood, picked up their weapons and began stowing them in kit bags.

"You mean we have to stay here? Indefinitely?"

The man turned and glared at him. "Do you have a problem with that?"

"No... well... I had plans this evening."

The other men sniggered and from the corner of his eye, Danny could see Yu-Ming shaking his head.

The older man stepped closer and jabbed a finger in Danny's chest. "Forget about your plans. This is the most important thing you can do. You're being paid and you're serving the motherland. You might have been born here, but you are Chinese. It's your duty to serve your country."

Danny gulped and averted his gaze. "Yes... Okay."

"Good." The man turned and barked another instruction, and the men hoisted their bags on their shoulders and headed for the door.

The older man, still standing in front of Danny, turned and looked at Yu-Ming. He said something, Yu-Ming nodded, then with one last glare at Danny, he followed his men to the door.

A minute later, Yu-Ming and Danny were standing alone in the empty warehouse.

"Who were they?" Danny asked.

"I think *Guojia Anquan Bu.*"

"What's that?"

Yu-Ming shook his head. "You really are a *lao wai*. *Guojia Anquan Bu* is the Ministry for National Security."

"So those men work for the Chinese Secret Service?"

"Probably. The van had embassy plates."

"Probably? You mean you don't know? What were you talking about in Mandarin?"

"I told them who we were and that we'd been told to report here for duty."

"And they didn't tell you anything?"

Yu-Ming shrugged. "No, but how does it matter? We were told to come here and we have. Now we have to do what they said."

"Those guys had guns, Yu-Ming." Danny pointed at the shipping container. "And there's a prisoner in there. I thought we were just being paid to watch a *lao wai*?"

"Well, now the job has changed." Yu Ming grinned. "You said you were bored with sitting in that apartment. Now you're doing some proper work."

Danny frowned. What had he got himself into?

29

Archibold Cholmondeley-Warner eased the phone back onto the cradle and placed both hands palm down on the leather surface of his desk. He stared at his manicured fingernails, not seeing them but running back over the conversation he had just had on the telephone.

Curious. Very curious. He lifted his hands, placed the fingertips together and steepled them together under his chin, then closed his eyes.

A kidnapping in the Hampshire countryside. A Portuguese journalist. Chinese nationals. Private aircraft. Very curious.

Opening his eyes, he pressed a button on the intercom and called out, "Mary, be a dear and bring me the file for that thing that happened in Winchester last year. The one in that beautiful house..."

"The Atwell Estate?"

"Yes. That's the one. Oh, and a cup of tea while you're at it."

He let go of the intercom button and sat back in his

chair, crossing one elegantly tailored suit leg over the other. It was all coming back to him now. The affair had stuck out because the former owner of the estate, Pinky Atwell, had gone to school with his father. The poor chap had fallen on hard times—a nasty gambling habit—and swallowed the twin barrels of his Purdy Side-by-Side. A beautiful gun, but it must have made a frightful mess.

What *had* made a frightful mess was the Chinese businessman who bought the estate for a song and then, with complete disregard for culture and tradition, altered and changed the house, which had stood for hundreds of years. A shudder ran down Archibold's spine. Ghastly! Heaven forbid someone would do that to Cholmondeley Manor.

When news broke about the Chinese owner's disappearance, his first thought had been good riddance. But when he heard reports of a gunfight, and rumors of blacked out helicopters arriving in the middle of the night, he had felt it prudent to pay the house a visit.

After three days of investigation, it was clearly apparent that a terrible crime had been committed. Any man who deemed it fit to install aluminium framed windows in the brick and flint walls of a Jacobean-era stable block should indeed be locked away for the rest of their life.

He let out a long sigh just as the door to his office opened and Mary walked in with a file under one arm and a mug of steaming tea in the other hand.

He ran a disapproving eye over the bright yellow mug with a smiley face on the side, then raised an eyebrow at his long-suffering secretary.

She placed the file on the desk and, still with the mug in her hand, matched his gaze unapologetically. "All the good china is in the dishwasher."

"The dishwasher?"

"Well, I'm sure you don't expect me to wash the cups."

"No, no, heaven forbid." Archibold shook his head. "What happened to the tea lady?"

"She resigned."

"Resigned. But she's been here for twenty years."

Mary shrugged, but said nothing.

"Oh, well." Archibold uncrossed his legs, sat forward and took the mug of tea from her. "Thank you."

"Will there be anything else?"

"No, that will be all, Mary... unless you can find us a new tea lady."

Mary said nothing, but the look she gave him would have struck fear into a lesser man. He waited until she closed the door behind her, before regarding the mug with distaste. What was the world coming to?

Putting his aversion to one side, he took a sip of the hot sweet liquid, and the world was on its way to being alright again.

Placing the mug on his desk, he turned it so he couldn't see the smiley face and flipped open the file.

The policeman, Sergeant Manners, was the one who proposed the connection. According to his theory, the chances of two separate incidents involving Chinese nationals occurring in the same area with no connection seemed highly improbable. Therefore, he believed there must be a link between them.

Archibold preferred to work with facts, but was inclined to agree with the man.

He slid the file closer, reached for the tea mug, took a sip, and began reading.

30

With his eyes on the driver, John said, "There's a big roll of cash lying on the floor in the back here. Maybe your last passenger dropped it?"

There was no response, and satisfied that the taxi driver didn't speak English, John settled back in his seat, pulled out his phone, and dialed Ramesh.

"I was about to call you, John."

"And?"

"The registration matches a silver Mercedes registered to the Chinese Consulate in Lisbon," Ramesh replied.

"A silver Mercedes? But the vehicle was a blue van."

"Yes. I know."

"So fake plates." John frowned. "What the hell does that mean?"

"I don't know, John. But my guess is they weren't really embassy staff."

"But whoever it is, they want Xie. They sent me a message. Xie for D'Silva."

"But Xie's dead... isn't he?"

John exhaled loudly. He stared out the window at the

passing countryside. "I don't know, Ramesh. I don't know. What do I do? How do I get her back?"

"John, there's something I've been meaning to tell you."

"What now?"

"I told Steve. He's coming to help you."

"What do you mean?"

"Exactly what I said. As soon as I told him about Adriana, he dropped everything and jumped on a flight. He'll be there… in about another four hours."

John was secretly relieved. Steve and he had been through a lot together in the past, and John knew he could always depend on the Australian ex-policeman.

"We're all here for you, John. Whatever you need, whatever it takes, you can depend on us."

"Thank you, Ramesh. I appreciate it." He took a deep breath. "I'm heading back home now, so send Steve the address. I'll be there in under an hour."

"Okay."

Neither of them said anything for a little while. John watched the countryside pass by while half listening to Ramesh typing on his keyboard.

"Ramesh, do you think you can track the phone that messaged me?"

"I can try."

"Good. I'll send you the number. It's the only lead we have right now."

"What are you going to do?"

"To be honest, I really don't know, Ramesh. I suppose I need to find out if Xie is still alive and then, if he is alive, convince the Nkuru Government to give him up."

"And if he's dead?"

"I'll cross that bridge when I come to it."

31

The taxi pulled up outside John's building and the driver glanced up at the rear-view mirror.

John ignored him and sat staring at the building entrance.

Just three days ago, he and Adriana had left the building on the way to England. Just three days, but it felt like a lifetime.

"*Senhor?*"

John snapped out of it. "*Sim. Obrigado.*" He removed a wad of cash from his wallet, counted out the fare, added a bit extra, and handed it over. "*Fique com o troco,* keep the change."

John climbed out of the car and stood on the sidewalk, staring at his reflection in the glass doors of the apartment building. He looked and felt ten years older. Taking a deep breath, he crossed the sidewalk and entered the building.

"*Boa tarde, Senhor* Hayes. You are back so soon."

John forced a smile and greeted the security guard. "*Boa tarde,* Miguel, yes, just a quick trip."

"And *Senhora* D'Silva?"

"She's coming back later." John lied, his eyes on the waving Chinese cat that still sat on the reception counter.

"Miguel, were you on duty four days ago? On the night shift?"

"*Sim Senhor. Por quê?* Why?" Miguel looked worried.

John smiled to put him at ease. "Nothing major. Just this cat." He gestured to the waving cat. "Where did it come from?"

"Oh yes, it's for good luck, no?" Miguel smiled, relieved he wasn't in trouble. "Someone came in and gave it to me. Said he was donating them to people. Told me he was *Budista...*"

"Buddhist?"

"*Sim. Budista.* So he was giving the cats away as a good deed. For... how you say in English... *ganhar merito?*"

"To gain merit."

"*Sim.*" Miguel nodded. "It looks nice, no?"

"Very nice," John agreed. "Can you describe the man? Was he Portuguese?"

"*Nao, nao,*" Miguel shook his head. Then a look of contrition crossed his face. "I mean yes, he spoke fluent Portuguese, but his face... he was *Chinês.*"

"Chinese?"

"*Sim, Senhor.*"

John stared at Miguel for so long Miguel had to look away. *A Portuguese speaking Chinese man.*

"Was he young or old?"

"Young." Miguel frowned. "Is something the matter, *Senhor*?"

"No, no, but I need a favor, Miguel."

"Anything *Senhor* Hayes."

John lowered his voice and leaned closer. "Can you show

me the security footage from that night? When the man came in?"

Miguel looked around the lobby, then up at the camera above the front entrance door. He shook his head.

John, anticipating this, had removed a hundred euro note from his pocket. He shifted position so his body was between the guard and the camera, and slid the note across the counter.

Miguel looked at it, then up at John.

"Give me your email address. I'll mail it to you."

"*Obrigado,* Miguel. As soon as you can."

Miguel pushed a notepad and pen towards John while deftly pocketing the money in one fluid motion, suggesting he had done it before.

John wrote his email address and handed it back.

"*É urgente*, Miguel."

"Right away, *Senhor*."

32

The apartment felt empty, as if it had lost its soul. John stood in the doorway, struggling against feelings of sadness and despair, despite his father's earlier encouragement.

Taking a deep breath, he stepped inside, closing the door behind him. He tossed the keys into the bowl on the console table beside the door, slipped off his shoes, and walked over to the kitchen. Taking a glass from the cupboard, he ran the tap, filled the glass with water, then gulped it down.

A wave of fatigue swept over him, as the adrenaline he'd been running on all day faded away and left him feeling spent. He'd been on edge since the kidnapping that morning.

Had it really been only that morning?

It felt like days ago. He refilled the glass, then leaned against the countertop. He hadn't eaten or had anything to drink since leaving his parents' home that morning. Feeling dehydrated but lacking appetite, he continued sipping water.

Once the glass was empty, he deposited it in the sink, then pulled out his phone and checked the screen. Still no reply.

In the taxi, he had placed a call to Joseph Tamba, the son of the President of the Democratic Republic of Nkuru. It had been months since their last contact, just before he had vanished into the night on the unmarked helicopter. John was uncertain if Joseph still used the number or would even reply, but he felt compelled to exhaust every option. However, the call went straight to voicemail, so he followed up with a text, hoping for a response. Eventually, things would fall into place and he would get Adriana back. Until then, he would pursue every avenue available to him.

The phone buzzed in his hand, sending a surge of excitement through his chest. Yet, it wasn't a message, but an email notification. He quickly opened it to find an email from Miguel, complete with a video attachment. Making his way around the kitchen, he settled onto a stool at the breakfast bar. Adjusting the phone horizontally, he tapped on the attachment.

A black and white video started playing, initially showing the reception desk, with Miguel seated behind it. Then, John noticed Miguel glancing up as a man entered the lobby. John peered closer, but the camera angle only revealed the back of the man's head. He was dressed casually in a hoodie, jeans, and running shoes, carrying a backpack over one shoulder. He spoke to Miguel for a while, then opened his backpack and pulled out the *Jiu Choi Maau*, placing it on the counter in front of him. The two men spoke for another minute, and then the visitor turned to leave.

John paused the video and zoomed in to the man's face. He was young, perhaps in his mid to late twenties... and Chinese.

John took a screenshot, then allowed the video to keep playing until the man disappeared from sight beneath the camera.

John examined the screenshot, zooming in and out, but he didn't recognize the man. But then, why would he?

With a sigh, he forwarded the video and the screenshot to Ramesh with a message to identify him, then placed the phone down on the countertop. He leaned his elbows on the counter and buried his face in his hands.

Could it be nothing more than a coincidence? Just chance that a Chinese man had donated the Chinese cat to the building? Maybe he truly was a Buddhist seeking to accumulate merit for a favorable rebirth?

Maybe Joseph Tamba would never call him back? Maybe Xie was dead anyway, so there was nothing he could do, and he would never see Adriana again.

He dug his fingers into his face, then clenched them into fists and slammed the countertop.

"Fuuuuuuuuuck!" He had to do something, had to get moving, anything to occupy his mind. If he sat around waiting for a call, he would sink further into a pit of depression that he would struggle to climb out of.

He spun around in his chair, his eyes falling on the bottles of gin on the silver tray on top of his liquor cabinet. He hesitated, then shook his head. Drinking wasn't the answer.

He slid off the chair. He was tired, his body hurt, he had a throbbing headache, but he'd go for a run instead. Hard physical activity would fix his mood.

34

Danny Chan cursed himself quietly. He'd slipped up. He'd wanted to keep his local identity secret. To most people, all Asians looked alike, and he wanted to take advantage of that. But now the prisoner knew he was Portuguese.

"*Merda!*" he cursed again, this time out loud.

"What happened?"

Yu-Ming was sitting with his feet up on a table, scrolling through his phone.

"Nothing. I... I ah... just remembered I'm supposed to pick something up for my mum, and I can't now."

The explanation seemed to work because Yu-Ming said nothing more and went back to his phone.

Danny walked over to the tables, picked up a bottle of water, and then emptied it into the kettle. He switched it on, removed a packet of instant noodles from one of the cardboard boxes stacked by the wall, and emptied the contents into a bowl.

As he waited for the kettle to boil, he glanced around the

warehouse. At the front, next to the entrance door, there was a basic office with grimy and cracked glass windows overlooking the warehouse. Next to it, there was a door leading to a single toilet, which Danny had already used. It stank of stale urine, and the toilet and washbasin were chipped and stained. Near the boxes of noodles and stacks of bottled water, there were two stained mattresses and a couple of rolled-up sleeping bags.

Danny wrinkled his nose in distaste as the kettle clicked off. He wasn't sure his situation was any better than when they had been in the apartment. At least the apartment was clean and had proper facilities. And he could walk home, sleep in his own bed, and eat home-cooked food. He didn't relish spending his days and nights in an empty warehouse, eating instant noodles, with Yu-Ming, who snored and farted in his sleep.

He turned around and poured hot water over the noodles and then stirred them with a pair of disposable chopsticks.

"How long do you think we have to stay here?" he asked.

Yu-Ming shrugged. He was intently watching a video with a Chinese language soundtrack.

Danny sighed, walked to a chair and sat down, the bowl of noodles in one hand and the chopsticks in the other. He took a noisy slurp of noodles, and was surprised to find them quite tasty. Nothing like a good dose of flavour enhancers to make rehydrated food taste good.

He studied the rusty and dented shipping container while he ate. The name of a Scandinavian shipping company was just legible on the side in faded white lettering.

He recognized the prisoner. He'd been watching her

apartment for the last six months. But seeing her up close was still a shock.

All this time, he had thought the man was the target, but it was the woman. Why? What had she done? She didn't seem threatening. She definitely didn't look like a criminal. In fact, she was quite striking. Olive skin under a thick mane of glossy black hair, and eyes that made his heart skip a beat when she looked at him.

"Do you know who she is?" he asked over his shoulder, but all he got in reply was a grunt.

Danny sighed. Yu-Ming never seemed to question anything, as if his only role in life was to follow orders from his superiors. Was that what they did to you in China? Brainwashed you into blind obedience? Danny frowned. Was that why his parents left and came to Portugal? He'd never discussed it with them, just taken it for granted. They always spoke of China in glowing terms and complained about how living with the whites was not like living back in China. But if it was so bad here, why didn't they go back?

Danny shrugged and slurped another mouthful of hot noodles. He didn't consider himself Chinese unless he looked in the mirror. He liked the food, but he didn't speak the language, and all his friends were Portuguese. He'd had to assimilate as much as possible, being the only Asian in his school, and he'd worked hard to make sure he was as Portuguese as everyone else.

He licked his lips and thought about the prisoner again. What had this lady done? She'd obviously upset someone. Danny sniffed and wiped his mouth with the back of his hand. Anyway, overthinking wouldn't do him any good. He was getting paid, and as long as he wasn't doing anything too illegal, he'd just stay silent and continue accepting his weekly cash.

But somewhere deep inside, it didn't seem right.

He pushed the feeling aside and concentrated on the noodles.

35

John stepped out of the shower and toweled himself dry before tapping on the screen of his phone lying on the vanity unit. Still no messages. Frowning, he checked the time. He'd run for forty-five minutes, but there was still nothing from Tamba and not even a message from Ramesh. He wrapped a towel round his waist and walked into the bedroom, just as the intercom buzzed in the living room. Walking out, he pressed the answer button and said, "Yes?"

"*Senhor* Hayes. *Senhor* Steve is here."

"Send him up Miguel. *Obrigado*."

John hung up, unlocked the door, leaving it slightly ajar, then walked back into the bedroom and pulled on his pants and a shirt. By the time he was dressed, he heard the door open and a voice call out.

"Hi honey, I'm home."

John chuckled, all his worries temporarily forgotten. He walked out into the living room and grinned at his old friend.

"Steve, you old dog. I hate to say it, but it's really good to see you."

Steve unslung a leather holdall from his shoulder and deposited it on the floor. He grinned back. "The feeling's mutual, mate." He held up a bag with Dubai Duty Free emblazoned on the side. "Thought you might be thirsty."

John crossed the living room, gripped Steve's hand, then pulled him in for a hug. "Thanks, Steve. I really appreciate you coming."

Steve slapped him on the back a couple of times, causing John to wince, then pushed him away and held him at arm's length. He looked into John's eyes and his smile faded. "We'll get her back, mate. I'm not leaving until we do."

John nodded and looked away, his eyes welling with tears. He bent down, picked up Steve's bag, and cleared his throat. "Come, I'll show you your room."

He led Steve to the spare room and dumped his bag on the bed. "Do you want to freshen up? There are fresh towels in the bathroom."

"No, mate. Plenty of time for that later. Let's talk." He thrust the duty-free bag into John's hand. "Maybe over a drink. Here."

John took it and looked inside at the two bottles of Botanist gin. He took a deep breath and shook his head. "We'll open these when it's all over, Steve. Right now, I want a clear head. Coffee?"

"I'd love one."

36

John busied himself in the kitchen, grinding the beans and boiling water while Steve stood by the window looking out across the Lisbon skyline. The setting sun cast a golden glow, highlighting the orange hues of the terracotta rooftops..

"Great view mate. I've never been here before." He turned to look back at John. "I wish it was under better circumstances."

"Yeah," John sighed. "How's Maadhavi?" he asked, changing the subject.

"She's good, mate. Still dividing her time between Dubai and India. I can't keep up with her. Don't know how she does it."

John smiled. He was fond of the Indian actress who had become a good friend after he saved her from the clutches of Surya Patil.

He poured hot water over the freshly ground coffee in the French press, grabbed a couple of cups, and walked over to the dining table. "Four minutes."

Steve nodded, walked over, pulled out a chair, and sat

down, stretching his legs out, crossing them at the ankle, and leaning back.

"So... Ramesh gave me some background, but I want to hear it from you."

John nodded, walked around to the opposite side of the table and pulled out a chair for himself. He sat and stared at the French press. The run had helped put him in a better frame of mind; the endorphins making him forget his injuries and pushing away the black cloud of despair and depression. But now here sitting in front of his old friend, all the horrible thoughts and emotions threatened to come flooding back. He felt a lump in his throat and his eyes welled with tears of anger and frustration.

As if sensing what he was going through, Steve sat forward and leaned his thick sun freckled forearms on the table. "Hey, John. You're not alone. I'm here for you. Ramesh too. We'll find her."

John nodded and swallowed the lump away.

"Shit, mate, look at what we've dealt with before. Foreign fuckin' Legion, those bloody rag-heads in Syria..."

John started to feel better. "You're not supposed to call them rag-heads."

"ISIS mate. Calling them rag-heads is polite."

John grinned. Having Steve with him would help a lot. If only for the reassurance and camaraderie. He leaned forward and looked at his watch before depressing the plunger on the French press.

He poured two cups of coffee and slid one toward Steve. He took a sip of his own before setting the cup down on the table and looking at his friend.

"Right, so this is what happened."

The French press was empty by the time John had finished updating him. It wasn't just the events of the day but also the back story. Xie, his parents, the Atwell Estate, and Joseph Tamba.

Steve let out a low whistle. "Bugger me, mate, never a dull moment with John Hayes."

John shook his head. "If it was just me, it would be okay. But it always affects those I love."

Steve leaned back in his chair and stared at John, a slight frown on his forehead.

John matched his gaze, waiting for him to say something.

After a while, Steve gave a nod and said, "Right, let's get the hacker on the phone. Get him to do something useful for once in his sorry life."

37

Ramesh's face appeared on the laptop screen. He was engrossed in typing and glancing at another monitor. The room behind him was dimly lit, with the screen's glow casting shadows on his face, making him look older than his years.

"Hey, you bloody curry muncher. Look at the state of you. You need to get out and get some sun. You'll be whiter than me soon."

Ramesh grinned and faced the camera. "At least I'm not out shagging sheep."

"Don't knock it 'til you've tried it, mate. At least I'm getting some action."

John shook his head, but couldn't help smiling. These two constantly teased each other, but he knew if it came to it, they would give their lives for each other.

"Have you guys finished?"

"Sorry, John." Ramesh interlaced his fingers and turned his hands inside out, stretching his arms above his head. "I've had no luck with that phone number. It's an unregistered burner on the MEO network."

"That's the largest network here, so that's not a surprise," John replied.

"Yeah, and their online security is top-notch. I've been unable to track the phone."

"Damn."

"Sorry." Ramesh looked embarrassed at his failure.

"It's okay. I've still not got a call back from our African friend."

"Joseph Tamba." Ramesh noticed John's raised eyebrow and added, "don't worry, this line is secure. No-one can listen in, not even the Chinese."

"Good." John sighed. "He's now a senior minister in his father's cabinet, so I don't even know if the number I have is current or if my message will reach him. We'll just have to wait and hope for the best." John leaned back in his chair and folded his arms. "Anyway, this is what we know so far. Chinese kidnappers took Adriana and transported her to an unknown location here in Portugal. They claimed diplomatic immunity when questioned by the local authorities, but the van had fake diplomatic plates. And I've received a text stating Adriana will be exchanged for Xie. Have I missed anything?"

John glanced at Steve and Ramesh as they both shook their heads.

"So what do we do? No suggestion is too stupid right now."

Both men remained silent while John chewed his lip.

Eventually, Steve broke the silence. "Why would they have fake diplomatic plates on the van if they were actually diplomats?"

John turned down the corners of his mouth and shrugged.

"Which would suggest they aren't working for the embassy," Steve finished the thought.

"Yup."

"So then, who's behind it? If not, the government...?"

"It has to be someone who was around when Xie disappeared." Ramesh piped up.

"The woman," John replied.

"Who?" both Ramesh and Steve asked at the same time.

"His assistant. She questioned me. One time when I went onto the estate to meet Xie." John frowned, recalling the events of the final night when Xie was 'disappeared.' "I never saw her again. She just vanished, and then..." he trailed off.

"Then what, John?" Steve leaned closer, watching John intently.

John exhaled loudly. "I got a text that evening when I got back to the motel... after everything was over." He looked up at Steve. "From an unknown number."

"What did it say?"

"Nothing. It was a picture. A picture of a *Jiu Choi Maau.*"

"What the fuck is that?"

"One of those waving Chinese cats."

"What? The ones people buy for good luck?"

"Yeah." John sighed.

Steve looked confused.

"Just like the one found in your apartment?" Ramesh asked from the computer.

"Exactly."

"Shit. Why didn't you tell me?"

"I... I don't know. I guess I was just glad everything was over."

Steve was looking from John to the screen and back, following the exchange with complete confusion.

"Will someone please explain what's going on?"

"One of those cats was left inside... *inside,* Steve," Ramesh emphasized, "inside the apartment you're in right now while Adriana was sleeping."

"What? When?"

"While all the Xie stuff was going on," John answered quietly.

"So someone broke into this apartment and left a waving cat?"

John nodded.

"And then sent you a picture of another one when you got rid of Xie?"

"And someone left another one in the lobby of John's building four days ago," added Ramesh.

"Fuck!"

John nodded again.

"But what does it mean?"

John shrugged. "I don't know the significance of the cat. But it's obviously the same person or people as back then, and they're trying to intimidate me. Showing me they can get to me at any time."

Steve exhaled loudly through pursed lips, folded his arms and sat back, shaking his head.

After several moments of silence, he asked, "So you think it's this Chinese woman?"

"I can't think of anyone else."

"Can we find her?"

John shrugged and glanced at Ramesh on the screen.

Ramesh made a face. "I need something to work on. Do you at least have a name?"

"Wang something..."

"Well, that narrows it down."

"There must be something in the company records... ummm Golden Fortune, I think that's the name. It's been wound up, but there must still be something online. Do you think you can find it?"

Ramesh had already turned his attention to the other monitor and was typing away rapidly. John waited patiently, confident that if anyone could find the information, Ramesh could.

"Is there a Chinatown here?"

John glanced over at Steve. "Yeah, *Martim Moniz*. It's not far."

"Maybe I can ask around? Find out where you can buy a waving cat?"

John made a doubtful face, but then had an idea. He grabbed his phone and scrolled through the photos, finding the screenshot of the young Chinese man who had delivered the cat to his lobby. "This guy. Try to find this guy." He showed Steve the screen. "I'll forward it to you."

"Do people speak English here? My Portuguese is as good as my Chinese."

"Your English isn't much better," Ramesh's voice came from the laptop speaker. Before Steve could retort, he added, "I've found her." A photo appeared on the screen. A middle-aged woman with a bad haircut and thick-rimmed glasses.

"That's her."

"She's a beauty. Looks like your type, Ramesh."

"Baaaa," Ramesh countered.

"Guys, focus," John interjected. "What's her name?"

"Wang Mingmei. Says here that she is... was... Xie's executive assistant."

"Yes, that's her. See if you can find out what she's doing now."

"I'm on it." Ramesh continued typing.

John picked up his phone and opened the message he'd received from the burner. He thought for a moment, then tapped on the number and dialed.

Steve was watching him. "Who are you calling?"

"I'm not sure, but my guess is Wang Mingmei."

38

Wang Mingmei sipped her hot oolong tea, while gazing out at the sun setting on the overgrown garden of the farmhouse. She found no joy in the reddening sky or the evening birdsong from the cork trees at the edge. Instead, she replayed in her mind the events of the day. She had devoted three months to careful planning, preparing for every eventuality and so far it had gone smoothly.

The sudden cutback in funding and support from her superiors at the *Guojia Anquan Bu* was an unexpected setback, but one she had soon dealt with. She still had control over several of Golden Fortune's secret offshore accounts. Accounts that even the insolvency administrators wouldn't find, so money wasn't an issue.

Dealing with the reduction in manpower had posed a greater challenge, but Wang Mingmei tapped into her network of less reputable organizations operating worldwide. organizations that operated on the other side of the law but who were often used by the Chinese Communist

Party to carry out deniable operations. She had called in a favor from the *Sun Yee On* Triad in the former Portuguese colony of Macau. During Golden Fortune's construction of a casino, the *Sun Yee On* had taken the labor contract, importing workers from impoverished areas of the mainland. It had been lucrative for both parties and they owed her a favor. That debt plus a hefty transfer of funds from a numbered account in Panama had guaranteed the supply of manpower for the kidnapping - a *Bai Leng*, a seasoned enforcer, and three *Xiao Di*, junior foot soldiers. They had come from France and had been worth every penny, the kidnapping going off without a hitch.

But for the next phase of the operation, she only needed someone to watch the prisoner and wait for instructions. The two men, the junior *Guojia Anquan Bu* staffer from China and the local boy, were more than sufficient.

She finished her drink, set the cup on the tray, and rose from her seat. The temperature had dropped noticeably as the sun dipped below the horizon. Carrying the tray, she made her way back inside.

The farmhouse was owned by an untraceable shell company, one of many properties she had purchased using offshore funds diverted from Golden Fortune. Other than installing fast internet, a security system, and making the kitchen functional, she had spent little on the property. The goal was to avoid attracting attention, and to outsiders, the building looked like many other stone farmhouses gradually decaying over time.

She placed the tray on the kitchen table, then entered her office. Standing before a flat-screen monitor, she studied the black-and-white feed from a camera positioned high on the wall of the warehouse in Abrunheira.

Yu-Ming sat with his feet up on the table, scrolling through his phone, while the local boy, Chan, walked around the warehouse with his hands in his pockets. She tapped a command on the keyboard and the camera zoomed in toward the shipping container, giving her a closer view of the door. It was locked. Satisfied, she straightened up and checked the thin gold watch on her wrist. Now all she had to do was wait.

She glanced around the room at its cluttered walls. Not a surface was free. Every inch covered in paper, maps, and surveillance photos. Seven months of tireless effort, following leads, encountering dead ends, and chasing false trails. She had combed the English countryside, scoured the internet, called in favors, contacted associates all over the world, and spent much of her time in Africa, pursuing one lead after another.

Behind the computer monitor, in the centre of the wall, was a large framed portrait of the man she was seeking. The man she secretly loved, Xie Longwei. A lone tear trailed down her cheek as she spoke to the photo, as if he were present in the room with her. "I will find you."

She regretted not dealing with the wretched Englishman permanently when she'd had a chance. That day in her office, when her security men had brought him in. She exhaled slowly, attempting to control her anger as the memories came flooding back. That was the day the Devil had entered her life.

She continued staring at the photo, turning the anger into determination, just as she had done every day for the last seven months.

"I will find you, *qin'ai de*, my darling, and when I do, I'll make sure the *lao wai* will suffer as much as I have."

Her plan would work, she was sure of it.

The buzzing of a phone brought her back to the present, and she glanced down at the row of cell phones on the desk in front of the monitor.

Her heart leaped into her throat.

The *lao wai* was calling.

39

Archibold Cholmondeley-Warner paused in the doorway of the Travelers Club smoking room, adjusting his tie as he surveyed the occupants. He disliked the smell of tobacco and rarely visited this part of the club, but he knew he would find the man he was looking for inside.

He spotted him in a far corner, deep in conversation with another man of the same nationality, a thick shroud of smoke lurking above their heads.

"Good evening, Sir."

"Good evening, Watson." Archie smiled at the black-tie clad waiter hovering nearby. "A glass of my usual, please."

"But of course, Sir." Watson dipped his head and hurried off to fetch the drink.

Archie weaved his way between the clusters of leather armchairs and sofas, nodded at the Nigerian ambassador, avoided eye contact with the dreadful Bosnian mining baron, and called out a greeting to one of his old classmates from Eton. "Dickie, old chap, how's the knee?"

"Can't complain, Chummers. Won't be playing squash for a while, though."

Archie arranged his face in an appropriate expression of sympathy and continued, approaching the two middle-aged Chinese men in the corner. He fought the urge to sneeze as the cloud of smoke enveloped him, exacerbated by the pungent scent of the *Hongtashan* cigarettes they were smoking.

He put on a smile and cleared his throat.

"Anson, what a surprise. How are you?"

Anson Liu of the *Zhōngguó Wàijiāobù*, the Ministry of Foreign Affairs for the People's Republic of China, looked up, blinked twice, then smiled. "Archibold, how nice to see you again."

His accent was upper-class English, befitting a man educated at the same schools as Archibold. He stood, straightened the jacket of his immaculate Savile Row suit, and extended his hand.

Archibold shook it, smiling broadly, and asked, "How's Celia and the boys? They're both at Harrow, aren't they?" Archibold was well aware of the school Anson's sons attended. He had studied his file before entering the Club.

"They're all well. I'm impressed with your memory."

Archibold made a dismissive gesture with his hand. "You must all come to the house one weekend."

"That would be nice, thank you."

Archibold glanced down at Anson's companion, who remained seated, puffing on a cigarette—just one of many, judging by the overflowing ashtray on the table.

Anson made no effort to introduce him and Archie made a mental note to check the Club's register on the way out and find out who his guest was.

Before the silence became too uncomfortable, Archie

leaned closer and, with a broad smile still plastered across his face, asked in a low voice, "While I'm here, do you think I might have a word?"

A shadow passed briefly across Anson's face, quickly replaced by a smile... of sorts.

He said something in Chinese and his companion stubbed out his cigarette, stood up, silently buttoned his jacket and walked away.

Archibold watched him leave, then without waiting for an invitation took the recently vacated chair. Loosening his jacket, he crossed one leg over the other and flicked away an imaginary speck of dust from his suit pants. He waited until Anson returned to his seat before looking up. Just as he was about to speak, Watson materialized beside him, offering a tumbler of scotch on a silver tray.

"Oh, thank you, Watson." He glanced over at Anson. "Can I get you anything?"

Anson shook his head.

Archie took a sip of whisky, licked his lips appreciatively, then set the glass on the arm of the armchair. After a pause, he looked up. "Earlier today, three men of Asian ethnicity kidnapped a Portuguese national. The Portuguese national, a reputed journalist by the name of Adriana D'Silva, was then loaded onto a private aircraft and flown to Portugal."

Anson arched an eyebrow. "What on earth are you talking about?"

Archie gave him a meaningful stare, then took another sip of whisky before continuing. "Upon arrival in Portugal, the plane was met by Portuguese law enforcement. However, the passengers on the aircraft claimed diplomatic immunity, carried Chinese passports, and left in a van registered to your embassy in Lisbon." Archie looked pointedly at Anson. "Do you have anything to say about this?"

Anson narrowed his eyes and took his time to answer. "I have absolutely no idea what you're talking about and even if I did, what makes you think this has anything to do with me or the Ministry of Foreign Affairs?"

Archie huffed and studied the glass in his hand. Without looking up, he said, "What makes it even more interesting is the kidnapping happened just up the road from the Atwell Estate." He raised his gaze and looked Anson in the eye. "You probably remember the place? The previous owner, one of your citizens, disappeared about six or seven months ago. Under very suspicious circumstances."

Anson pushed out his lower lip and shrugged.

"The kidnapped journalist reported extensively on the owner of the estate, Xie Longwei, former Chairman of the now defunct Golden Fortune Corporation. Surely that must ring a bell?"

Silence.

Archie examined his glass once more, swirling the amber liquid around, before lifting it to his lips and finishing its contents. Leaning forward, he placed the glass on the table, his expression now devoid of any trace of a smile. He fixed Anson in a steely glare and spoke in a low tone, "I would hate to think you're running an operation in my backyard without informing me, old chap. That would be very bad form, and you know that sort of thing never ends well."

He sat back and smiled. "Anyway, I must be off. Places to be, things to do. You know how it is." He stood up and buttoned his jacket. "You'll keep me posted, won't you, old chap?" He winked. "Give my regards to Celia."

Without waiting for an answer, he turned and made his way out of the room, pausing only to shake hands with the Defense Attaché from Mozambique on the way out.

40

Anson Liu watched Archibold leave, barely able to contain his anger.

He despised being placed in an awkward situation, especially within the confines of the Club. What truly irked him, however, was his genuine confusion regarding Archibold's remarks.

He recalled the incident regarding Xie. It had caused a major storm in government circles, and he had narrowly escaped being reassigned to China. Anson was committed to serving his homeland, but had no inclination to return and reside there permanently. He had been educated at the finest schools in England and had since spent much of his adult life here. Although loyal to a fault, he was more English than Chinese, and much preferred the lifestyle and culture of his adopted homeland. He intended to keep it that way and could ill afford another embarrassing incident like the disappearance of Xie Longwei.

Anson composed himself, bottled his anger, and made his way toward the exit, nodding politely to his left and right, as he weaved between the tables.

His colleague was standing outside smoking, and when Anson appeared on the top step, he stubbed out the cigarette and raised his hand, signaling to someone unseen. By the time Anson reached the sidewalk, a sleek black Mercedes with diplomatic plates had pulled up at the curb.

Anson got into the back seat while his colleague settled in beside him on the other side. Once the doors shut and the car started moving, Anson turned to his colleague and asked, "Are we running anything at the moment?"

"Just the usual. Nothing new."

Anson glared at him. "How about the kidnapping of a journalist in Hampshire?"

Chen Wei shook his head, clearly puzzled.

Anson faced the front. Wei had confirmed what he already knew. For Anson Liu wasn't actually with the Ministry of Foreign Affairs for The People's Republic of China. That's just what his business card said. Anson Liu was the UK Chief of Intelligence for the Chinese Ministry for National Security. The *Guojia Anquan Bu*.

And the *Guojia Anquan Bu* no longer had an interest in Xie Longwei.

The Chinese Communist Party were a pragmatic bunch. If there was nothing to be gained from a situation, then their efforts were best focused elsewhere. There was certainly no benefit in pursuing the whereabouts of a businessman whose reputation had been tarnished in the international press after his disappearance. They had already washed their hands of the whole business.

Which meant only one thing.

The woman.

41

The call went unanswered so John dialed again. Placing the phone on speaker, he set it on the table between himself, Steve, and the laptop. The three men waited and listened, but there was still no answer.

John thumped the table. "Shit."

"What would you have said if she had answered?" Steve asked.

John shrugged and shook his head. "No idea." He screwed up his face and thumped the table again. "But at least it would have felt like I'm doing something."

Steve nodded and glanced at the laptop. Ramesh paused his typing, briefly looked in their direction, then returned his attention to the monitor. When no one spoke, he said, "She seems to have disappeared. I can't find any record of her after Xie's disappearance. It's as if she's vanished into thin air."

John buried his face in his hands. There had to be something he could do. He wasn't prepared to give up.

His phone vibrated with an incoming message and he snatched it off the table and peered at the screen.

"What is it?" Steve asked.

John turned the screen so both Steve and Ramesh could see the message.

Xie for D'Silva.

"The same message as before," John explained with a shake of his head.

"You're getting another call, John," Steve interrupted just as John felt the phone vibrate in his hand. He turned the screen to face him. "Joseph Tamba," he exclaimed, then held a finger to his lips, warning Steve and Ramesh to be silent.

Answering the call, he put it on speaker for all to hear.

"Joseph?"

"John Hayes, how are you doing? It's been a while."

John hadn't spoken to Joseph in over six months, but his deep, rich voice was instantly familiar.

"It has. Thank you for calling back. I wasn't sure if you were still using this number."

"I have many numbers now, John." Joseph chuckled. "Since we last met, my life has changed beyond all recognition."

"I know. I've been following your progress in the news. Minister of Defense now. I guess the time at Sandhurst wasn't a waste, after all."

"Cut short, John, as you know, but no experience is ever wasted."

"I agree. Well, I'm very happy for you, Joseph." John paused, not sure how he should continue.

Joseph's deep voice filled the gap. "And you, John? Is everything okay? Is your parents' house complete?"

"Soon, Joseph, soon. I'm estimating another couple of months before they can move in."

"That's good. I'm glad everything turned out okay in the end."

John looked up at Steve and grimaced. "Well, not quite, Joseph."

"I had a feeling this wasn't just a courtesy call."

"No, Joseph, I wish it was. I... I need to ask you something.... I don't know how secure your line is, so please bear with me. Do you remember our friend?"

"The line is secure, and yes."

"Is he... is Xie, still alive?"

There was a long silence, and John looked from Steve to Ramesh. Ramesh had stopped typing and was leaning back in his chair, observing and listening.

Eventually, Joseph replied, "Why do you ask?"

John leaned forward so his face was closer to the phone on the table. "This morning, three Chinese men kidnapped my girlfriend from next to my parents' house. They flew her in a light aircraft to a private airstrip in Portugal, where we've now lost track of her."

"Oh."

"Yes."

"Okay... I'm... I'm really sorry to hear this, John, but what makes you think it's connected to our friend?"

"Because I've since received a text message saying 'Xie for D'Silva.'" John paused and then added for clarity, "D'Silva is my girlfriend's name."

"I see."

There was again a long silence. The three men exchanged glances but remained silent, waiting for Joseph to respond.

"It pains me to say this, John, but I don't really see how I can help you. Have you contacted the police?"

John snorted, "Come on..." He took a breath, composing himself, and started again. "If I wait for the police, I'll never get her back."

"Hmmm."

John waited and when an immediate reply was not forthcoming he asked, "Look, Joseph, I didn't want to call in a favor, but if he's still alive, please give him up. This is the woman I love, the woman I want to spend the rest of my life with. This whole thing has nothing to do with her."

Again, there was silence. Frustrated, John looked up at Steve and shook his head.

"John... I... my country... owes you a great debt. I know that. But I'm afraid there's nothing I can do. Xie no longer exists."

"Fuck!" John couldn't help himself. He pushed back the chair and sprang to his feet. "Fuck, fuck, fuck!"

"I'm so sorry, John." Joseph's voice boomed from the phone's speaker.

John ignored him, shaking his head and pacing up and down. Steve caught his eye and then gestured toward the phone.

John paused in his pacing, said, "Thank you, Joseph," and signaled for Steve to end the call.

42

Danny yawned and glanced at his watch. It was time for Yu-Ming to check on the prisoner. A loud snore echoed around the empty warehouse space and he turned to see Yu-Ming, asleep with his head on his arms on the table.

Danny shook his head. Yu-Ming could sleep through anything, and the constant diet of instant noodles probably didn't help with his energy levels. He sighed and pushed back his chair. He'd do it himself this time and ensure Yu-Ming owed him.

He got up and stretched, arms reaching up, feeling his back pop and click as he straightened up. He rolled his head around, loosening his neck, then shook out the stiffness in his legs. Boredom and frustration from the lack of action were getting to him. If it weren't for the good pay and the absence of other job options, he would really think about quitting.

He went to the food storage area and picked up two water bottles, then headed to the shipping container. Holding the bottles under his left arm, he used his right hand to pull the lock open. The door made a grinding noise as it swung open, and he looked inside.

The woman was sitting in the corner on the mattress, hugging her knees to her chest. She watched him as he entered, but didn't speak. Danny was surprised by how calm she was. If he were in her shoes, kidnapped and locked in a shipping container, he'd be shitting himself. Yet, she appeared surprisingly at ease.

He tossed the water bottles onto the floor, watching them roll toward her, then bent down to pick up the empties. His nose wrinkled at the smell of urine and he glanced at the bucket. He'd make Yu-Ming empty it as a punishment for sleeping through his shift.

"*Qual o seu nome?*" Her voice broke the silence. "What's your name?"

Her question caught him off guard.

"I know you speak Portuguese," she continued.

Danny swallowed and backed toward the door.

"Do you know who I am?"

Danny paused in the doorway and shook his head.

"My name is Adriana D'Silva. Google me."

Danny quickly shut the door and looked over at Yu-Ming, who was still fast asleep. Danny threw the empty water bottles onto the trash pile in the corner, then stood with his hands on his hips, staring at the shipping container.

Why would she say that? Google me. Walking over to the table, he grabbed his phone and opened the browser. Typing in her name, he waited for the results to load. The sheer number of results surprised him. He scrolled through them, occasionally tapping on a link and skimming through the articles. *Award-winning Portuguese journalist... Público newspaper... Articles on the war in Syria... sex trafficking in an Indian ashram... exploitation of the Rohingyas in Thailand.*

One link caught his eye, and after another quick glance at Yu-Ming, he sat down to read further. It wasn't the first time she'd been kidnapped. Perhaps that's why she seemed so relaxed? She had been held hostage by ex *Légion étrangère* mercenaries in Oman. He read on, fascinated by the account of her previous kidnapping while on vacation and the daring rescue by another tourist.

But why would she be kidnapped again, and this time by the Chinese Government? He searched again, this time for her name along with the word 'China.'

Ten minutes later, he was even more confused. Her most recent articles related to China dated back half a year, focusing on exposing the corrupt practices of a company named Golden Fortune, a Chinese-owned construction firm involved in global infrastructure projects. However, that was all in the past; the company had since been dissolved, and its owner had vanished under mysterious circumstances, presumably because of financial troubles.

But that still didn't explain why she had been kidnapped now.

He turned in his chair and looked at Yu-Ming, who had changed position and was now leaning back in his chair, his head flung back, his mouth open, but still snoring.

Danny frowned. He had always been curious, bordering on nosy. It had got him in trouble before and he'd tried to rein in his tendency to pry where he shouldn't. But this was now eating away at him. He had to find out why this beautiful Portuguese woman was being held captive in a shipping container by the Chinese Communist Party.

Slowly he slid back his chair, trying to make as little noise as possible, and stood up. Walking over to the shipping container, he eased down on the handle, wincing at the creak and grind of the locking mechanism.

Danny cracked open the door and peered inside. She was sitting in the same position and when he caught her eye, she smiled.

She really was beautiful.

He looked back at Yu-Ming, then stepped inside and eased the door closed behind him.

"*Você é jornalista,*" he said. "You are a journalist."

"*Sim,*" she replied. "You googled me."

Danny nodded.

"Where am I?"

Danny frowned but didn't answer.

"I know I'm in Portugal." She reached forward and picked up a water bottle and held it so the label was visible. "*Luso.*"

Danny hesitated. He wanted to know more, but also didn't want to give anything away.

"Why are you here?" he asked finally.

She studied him for a while with her head tilted to one side, then asked a question of her own, "You mean you don't know?"

Before he could answer, he felt the door move behind him. Turning around, his face reddened with guilt as Yu-Ming, frowning, opened the door wide. Yu Ming glanced past him at the woman, then with a jerk of his head, signaled for Danny to leave the container.

Danny stepped outside, and Yu-Ming shut the door behind him.

"What are you doing?" he demanded.

"I was giving her some water." Danny replied hastily, worried about how much Yu-Ming had heard. He went on the attack. "It was your turn, but you were asleep. You owe me now."

It was Yu-Ming's turn to look uncomfortable. He

shrugged and looked away. "Okay. I'll do a double shift now."

Danny let out a sigh of relief. "Good, because I'm going out. I'm sick of sitting around in here."

"But we've been told to stay here."

Danny shrugged. "Well, I need something to eat other than instant noodles. I want some proper food."

"You'll get something for me?" Yu-Ming asked hopefully.

"Do a triple shift and I'll get whatever you want."

Yu-Ming didn't even hesitate. "Done."

43

Joseph Tamba walked around to the driver's side of the black Land Rover Defender and gestured to the driver to get out.

"Sir?"

"I don't need you."

The driver glanced nervously from Joseph to the uniformed aide-de-camp standing behind him.

Joseph arched an eyebrow. "Is there a problem?"

The driver snapped to attention and saluted. "No, Sir." He moved aside but still glanced nervously at the aide-de-camp, who cleared his throat and stepped forward.

"I don't need you either," Joseph said as he climbed into the Land Rover.

The aide-de-camp seemed like he was going to speak, then decided against it, nodded, stood at attention, and saluted.

Joseph closed the door, slipped the SUV into drive and pulled out of the portico. He flashed his lights, signaling for the guards to open the gates, slowing just enough for one of the armed guards to step into the road outside and block the traffic.

Joseph understood why his driver and aide-de-camp hesitated to let him go out alone. Protocol required him to always be accompanied by an armed bodyguard, and his driver was trained in defensive driving. But Joseph wasn't concerned. Since his father, the President of the Democratic Republic of Nkuru, had taken charge, the country had seen significant improvements. Domestic adversaries were non-existent, and the era of foreign colonial powers stirring unrest was over. The economy was booming, with profits being reinvested locally instead of being sucked offshore. Policies had been put in place to ensure free education and healthcare, and for the first time in years, people believed in their future.

However, Joseph, as Minister of Defense, didn't take his responsibilities lightly. While Africa was moving away from foreign dominance, any hint of weakness could attract outside interference, particularly in a resource-rich country like Nkuru. Therefore, Joseph maintained the military's readiness, just in case. He didn't expect trouble, but he kept a Glock strapped to his waist, and he knew how to handle himself. He had served in his country's special forces and had even been trained by the British before the Xie incident cut his training short.

As he navigated his way through the traffic, he thought back to the phone call with John Hayes. It had hurt him to say what he had. His country owed John Hayes a great debt. Xie Longwei and his corrupt practices had posed a serious threat to the freedom of the people of Nkuru. Initially, Golden Fortune's proposal for the development of Nkuru's port had seemed enticing. However, upon closer inspection, it became apparent that it was riddled with traps and penalties designed to enslave the people of Nkuru for generations, and granting the People's Republic of China economic control over the nation.

Because that's who Xie really worked for. The CCP.

And that was why no-one should ever know about Nkuru's involvement in Xie's disappearance..

As Joseph approached the outskirts of Zalendi and entered an industrial area, the traffic thinned out. The road conditions worsened, marked by numerous potholes and ruts caused by the frequent passage of heavy vehicles. Joseph reduced his speed, carefully navigating around the larger potholes, and made a mental note to discuss the road's condition with his colleague in the transport ministry. Despite the rapid development of the country, there was still ample room for improvement in infrastructure.

Joseph pulled up in front of a steel gate set in a high concrete wall topped with coiled razor wire. There were no signs revealing what lay beyond the gate, but everyone in Nkuru knew what had once been there.

Under the previous administration, the infamous Gorombe Correctional Facility had housed political prisoners and 'enemies of the state.' But when Babatunde Tamba swept to power, he granted an amnesty to all political prisoners and emptied the prison. As far as the public was concerned, the prison had been abandoned, an empty monument to the oppressive regime that once ruled over them.

Joseph rolled down the window and glanced up at the camera positioned over the gate. Although he hadn't called ahead, his face was easily recognizable. He waited, continuing to gaze at the camera, until, with a click, the gate began rolling open on well-oiled tracks.

A black clad guard stepped out from the guardroom

beside the gate, a Heckler and Koch MP5 on a single point sling held at low ready. As the Land Rover entered, the guard stepped back and stood at attention, releasing his grip on the weapon and offering a crisp salute. Joseph acknowledged with a nod, then entered the compound and drove down the side of the building before pulling into a spot in front of an unmarked steel door.

He climbed out and paused in front of the door, looking up at another camera. There was the electronic whirring of locks and the door clicked open. He stepped inside, closing the door behind him, and greeted another guard standing to attention behind a large glass window to the left of the entrance. This guard too was dressed in black tactical clothing, a Glock holstered at his waist, and behind him a large bank of monitors displayed the black-and-white feed from the security cameras.

Joseph entered the room and asked, "Anything to report?"

"No, Sir. All quiet."

"Good." Joseph moved to the monitors and studied the feeds. One monitor displayed footage from the camera at the front gate, while others monitored the boundaries of the compound. Additionally, there was one positioned above the entry door to the prison. But the one that interested Joseph was the monitor in the centre. It showed a windowless cell with a steel toilet in one corner and a single bed built into the opposite wall. Apart from the w/c and the bed, there were no other furnishings, the room bare and harshly lit from the fluorescent tubes set into the ceilings.

There was a man sitting on the bed, now the sole occupant of the Gorombe prison. A heavy chain ran from a shackle around his ankle to a ring set high on the wall, the chain just long enough for the prisoner to move from the bed to the toilet.

"Zoom in closer," Joseph instructed, prompting the guard to step forward and tap on the keyboard. As the camera focused on the bed, Joseph leaned in, narrowing his eyes. The man appeared noticeably thinner, with sunken cheeks and dark circles under his eyes. The skin around his ankle was rubbed raw from the constant chafing of the shackle, and his feet were bare.

"Sound?"

The guard stepped forward once more and pressed a key, causing Joseph to flinch as the sound of "Baby Shark" playing on loop blasted out through the speakers. He couldn't imagine enduring that for twenty-four hours straight. Taking a deep breath, he felt a brief pang of guilt regarding the prisoner's treatment, but quickly dismissed it. Sometimes, difficult decisions had to be made for the greater good, and this was one of those times.

"Does he do anything?" Joseph asked the guard.

"No, Sir. Not anymore. He used to walk back and forth, but he's not done anything for a few months now."

Joseph nodded and leaned in closer, scrutinising the image on the screen. The man slumped on the bed, his chin resting on his chest, his hands resting in his lap. Though he seemed asleep, he suddenly lifted his head, as if sensing he was being observed, and stared at the camera.

Joseph gazed back at the haunted eyes of the man who had threatened to destroy the country he called his home.

Xie Longwei. A man who, to all intents and purposes, had ceased to exist.

44

John felt a wave of exhaustion wash over him and he slumped down in his chair. Leaning back, he closed his eyes and tried not to think. Thinking too much about the situation only brought him down, so he emptied his mind. He pushed aside thoughts of the day's events and the whereabouts of Adriana, choosing instead to surrender to the mental and physical fatigue in the hope of momentarily escaping reality.

John took a deep breath through his nose, exhaling slowly as he urged his body to unwind. With each inhale and exhale, he felt himself relaxing further, sinking deeper into the chair. A drowsiness crept over him, tendrils of sleep reaching out for him like grasping fingers. He had been on the go since early morning and even during the plane journey he had been on edge, draining him mentally and physically. Perhaps he could simply sleep it off? Maybe when he woke up, everything would have vanished, just like a bad dream.

He sank deeper into a drowsy state... then suddenly, a thought popped into his head, and he sat up.

"Let's plan the exchange."

Steve blinked in surprise. "What?"

John pulled the laptop closer, ensuring Ramesh heard everything. "Let's plan the exchange. Xie for Adriana."

"But... you heard what he said?" Steve looked extremely confused. "Xie doesn't exist anymore."

"We know that..." John nodded toward the phone on the table. "But they don't."

Steve didn't look convinced.

John turned to Ramesh on the laptop screen. He was leaning back in his chair, his fingers interlaced behind his head while he looked up at the ceiling.

"Let's agree to their demands and set up an exchange." John repeated.

"Where?" Ramesh asked.

"We'll work that out. But probably here somewhere," John replied, encouraged by Ramesh's response. "Because Adriana's here."

"And what happens when we turn up without Xie?"

John shrugged. "I don't know. I haven't thought that far ahead. Maybe we get an actor, someone who looks like him?"

Steve snorted. "Contrary to popular belief, John, they don't all look the same."

"You don't have to tell *me* that, Steve. But what else do we do? Sit around here hoping they'll give her back? No fucking way. At least we'll be moving forward. Maybe they'll make a mistake on the way and we'll be able to find out where she is?" John raised his hands. "Hell, I don't know. But at least we're doing something."

"I agree with John," Ramesh spoke up. "Let's get things moving. Try to force their hand."

John nodded and then looked at Steve for approval.

Steve massaged his face with his fingertips, then stretched his arms overhead. "Okay."

"Okay?"

"Okay." He nodded. "I'm in."

"Great!" John jumped up, excited, and began pacing around the room. "We'll need a good story. Where has he been all this time? Who had him?" He stopped pacing and turned back to face the table. "We'll need to stall them. Because it would be too much of a coincidence if he were being kept here in Portugal. They wouldn't believe that. So we need to allow time to get him here."

"We need to plan the handover. Needs to be somewhere that we can control. Because the minute they find out, it's not really Xie they will..." Steve trailed off, not wanting to voice his thoughts aloud.

John stared at him, his excitement fading as he completed Steve's sentence in his head.

He exhaled loudly and slumped back in the chair. He said nothing for a while, trying not to think about what would happen to Adriana if everything went wrong. Eventually, he looked up. "I still think we should do it. We'll make it work." He looked at Steve, then Ramesh. "We have to."

45

The sound of a buzzing phone in her office interrupted Wang Mingmei's cooking. She turned off the gas stove and headed to her desk. She stared down at the ringing phone with trepidation. It was her official phone, not a burner, and when her official phone rang, it usually wasn't good. She debated whether to ignore it, but decided the consequences of not taking the call could be worse, so she stepped forward and peered at the screen.

Liu!

She closed her eyes, took a deep breath, and picked up the phone.

"*Wei?*"

"Where are you?" Anson Liu growled.

Mingmei hesitated. Seven months ago, he would never have dared speak to her in this tone, but now she had fallen from grace. She considered lying, but knew Liu could trace the call before she even hung up.

"Portugal."

"And what are you still doing there? I thought we told you to wind up operations?"

"I'm tying up some loose ends."

"Really?" Liu's tone dripped with sarcasm.

Mingmei walked over to the window and stared out into the darkness, waiting for him to say something. She didn't have to wait long.

"This morning a Portuguese journalist was kidnapped from here in England by three Asian men and flown to Portugal."

Mingmei winced. It hadn't taken long for her superiors to make the connection. "Why are you telling me this?"

"Because I know it was you!" Liu exploded and Mingmei held the phone away from her ear while he continued, "Don't take me for a fool!"

Mingmei briefly considered denying it, but there was no point.

There was a long silence, and Mingmei hoped the call had cut out.

When Liu spoke again, his voice was cold and level. "This obsession has to stop. I told you to wind up this operation days ago. I can't protect you anymore, Mingmei. This has gone to the top. You're expected back in Beijing immediately."

Mingmei stared out the window. Her gaze moved from the farmyard to her reflection in the glass. She could see the lines of strain on her forehead, the dark smudges under her eyes. Her hair had thinned considerably and was now almost white.

"Do you understand?" Liu barked in her ear.

She swallowed and nodded at her reflection. "*Shi.* Yes."

"Immediately!" Liu repeated, and then the phone went silent.

Mingmei sighed and lowered the phone. She turned from the window and stared at the papers pinned to the walls. She wasn't going back to be shuffled off to some dead-end job in Xinjiang or Qinghai.

Her eyes fell again on Xie's photo. Without Xie her life was nothing. Looking down at the phone in her hand, she powered it down, removed the battery and the SIM, snapping the latter in two. She then tossed everything in the wastepaper bin. She would go dark if she had to, but she wasn't giving up on Xie. Mingmei was about to leave the room when one of the burners vibrated with an incoming message.

It was the burner she used to contact the *lao wai*.

Picking it up, she read the message on the screen.

Okay. But I need time to get him.

Intense emotion flooded through her, and she almost dropped the phone.

Finally.

She closed her eyes and said a silent prayer of thanks as a single tear rolled down her cheek.

46

The old grandfather clock in the corner of the office chimed the hour, and he glanced up to check the time.

Eleven p.m.

The clock had been with his family for three generations but still kept excellent time. Archie wasn't a fan of technology and he abhorred digital clocks. He preferred things the old-fashioned way. His only nod to technology was the computer on his desk and the cell phone, necessary evils, but ones he preferred to use as little as possible. His colleagues relied on data and the worst thing he'd ever heard of, artificial intelligence. But Archie preferred good old HUMINT, as the Yanks called it. Human intelligence. Nothing beat boots on the ground and conversations with real people. Looking someone in the eye and observing their body language taught you so much more than lines of code on a computer.

His office, too, reflected his way of thinking. Unlike his colleagues, who preferred formica and steel, he had furnished his office much like the interior of his club. Overstuffed leather chairs sat around a solid oak desk. Several paintings he had brought in from the country house adorned the walls, and on the floor was an ornate silk and wool rug his great grandfather had brought back from India. Archie spent most of his waking hours in the office, so it may as well be comfortable.

He sat back in his chair, unsnapped his gold cufflinks, and slipped them into the breast pocket of his shirt before rolling up his sleeves. It had been a long day, and he contemplated having a cup of tea. But Mary had gone home a long time ago, and he didn't know where she kept the teabags. Perhaps it was time for something stronger?

He stood, walked over to the crystal decanter on the sideboard and poured three fingers of scotch into a tumbler. Turning around, he leaned back against the sideboard and took a large mouthful. He held it in his mouth and savoured the peaty flavour on his tongue before swallowing. He sighed with satisfaction. It was a ten-year-old Ardbeg, peaty and smoky, with a hint of vanilla and much, much better than a cup of tea.

He carried it back to his desk and sat down, placing the glass beside the open file he had been studying for the past hour.

It was the second time he'd gone through it and he still couldn't figure out what the Chinese wanted with Adriana D'Silva.

Archie took another sip of whisky. He had been going back and forth in his head all evening trying to work out her connection with China.

His first thought had been the Triads, but there was nothing to suggest she was investigating any stories related to the Chinese crime syndicates

No matter which way he turned it, he kept coming back

to her work on Golden Fortune and the disappearance of Xie Longwei.

Could it be revenge? The Chinese were known to be patient. However, Archie had sat in a taxi outside the Travelers Club and watched Anson Liu leave. His body language suggested even he didn't know what was going on.

Archie flipped through the file once more, hoping an explanation would leap out at him. After a couple of minutes, he gave up, leaning back in his chair, nursing the tumbler of whisky in his lap. Someone had to know what was going on.

He raised the glass to his lips and drained the contents before setting the glass back on the table. As he did so, something in the file caught his eye and a lightbulb went off in his head. He reached for his cell phone, searched for a number, and dialed.

It took a while to be answered by a grumpy, sleepy voice.

"Hello?"

"Sergeant Manners." Archie glanced at the grandfather clock. "Is this an inconvenient time?"

"Ahhh..."

"Good. Archibold Cholmondeley-Warner here. Adriana D'Silva's boyfriend, Hayes. Do you have a number for him?"

Sergeant Manners cleared his throat and sniffed before answering, "Yes. Why?"

"Be a good chap and send it through, will you? I've got a few questions for him."

"Um... okay."

"Good chap."

"But he's not in England."

Archie frowned. "Not in England? I thought you interviewed him this morning?"

"I did. But since we spoke, he jumped on a plane to Portugal."

"Why didn't you tell me that earlier?"

"I... I didn't think it was important... for you to know."

"Oh... I see. Okay, well, send me that number as soon as you can."

"Do you think he's involved?"

"As soon as you can, old chap." Archie ignored him and ended the call.

So, your partner gets kidnapped, and suddenly you're hopping on a plane to Portugal. Intriguing.

Archie nodded to himself. This Hayes fellow definitely warranted further investigation.

He reached for the handset of the internal phone and pressed a number.

"Travel Desk."

"Oh yes, good evening. Can you get me on the first flight to Lisbon in the morning, please?"

47

John rubbed his tired eyes and leaned back in his chair. Steve looked back, his eyes red from fatigue. Only Ramesh appeared to have any energy left. They had been discussing the plan and backstory for hours, but had made no progress. Empty takeout boxes and dirty coffee cups littered the table, but the coffee had long stopped being effective.

John exhaled. "I think Ramesh is right. Let's base the story on the truth. It will be easier to remember, and why reinvent the wheel when we have a story already?"

"Blame it on the Africans?" Steve asked.

"Yes. Not Nkuru, though. We'll pick another country. Preferably one that Golden Fortune did business in. We'll say they've had him all along. They've agreed to release him, but it will take a couple of days to deal with the red tape and get him here."

Steve nodded slowly.

There was silence for a while, then Steve said, "We'll need time to find a location for the swap. Somewhere quiet, but a location we can control."

"They might already have a place in mind," Ramesh replied.

John shook his head. "No, we don't agree. So far, they've dictated things. We need to gain the upper hand, take control. We decide when and where."

"Yeah." Steve nodded in agreement.

John closed his eyes, visualising how he would want a swap to take place. Without opening his eyes, he said, "They're professional. The kidnapping was smooth and quick. There's at least four men, possibly more. They'll be armed and will probably have a shooter on over watch, ready to take us out..."

"Which they will once they know we don't have Xie."

John's eyes snapped open, and he stared back at Steve. "Yeah." He sighed loudly. "How the fuck do we do this? Even if we hire an actor to play Xie's role, they might kill him as soon as they realize he's not Xie." John shook his head. "I don't want that on my conscience, even to save Adriana." He shook his head again and thumped the dining table. "Fuck."

Steve turned his wrist and looked at his watch. "Why don't we call it a night? We're not getting anywhere and the more tired we are, the less we'll think clearly."

John pulled a face.

"John, there's nothing we can do right now. I know you're worried, but we need to rest. We'll solve this, but we'll make mistakes if we continue like we are now. We need clear heads."

"He's right, John. Let's get some sleep and return to this in the morning."

John glanced at the laptop. He hated the fact that he wasn't doing anything, and he felt guilty about sleeping comfortably in his own bed while Adriana was out there somewhere being held against her will. But the two men were right. He wasn't thinking straight.

"Okay," he sighed. "Let's get a couple of hours' sleep." He shrugged. "Hopefully, our subconscious will find a solution by the time we wake up." Leaning forward, his finger hovered over the keyboard. "I'll call you in the morning, Ramesh."

"Good night, John, and don't worry, we'll find her."

John nodded, then tapped the keyboard and ended the call.

Steve was watching him with concern. "We'll get her back, John. Believe it. I'm not leaving until she's back here safe and sound."

John stood up, walked around the table, and stopped beside Steve. Reaching out, he gripped Steve's shoulder and gave it a squeeze. "Thanks, mate. I appreciate it. I really do."

Steve reached up and patted his hand. "Everything will look better in the morning."

"I hope so, Steve. I hope so."

48

Mingmei drove the fifteen-year-old Volkswagen Golf into the compound and pulled up in front of the warehouse door. She waited for several minutes, her eyes on the rear-view mirror before turning off the engine and switching off the lights.

She had taken a circular route and was confident she hadn't been followed, but she had always been a cautious woman and old habits died hard.

She climbed out of the car and once more looked out through the gate to the street. The street was well lit but completely empty, all the surrounding businesses long closed for the night. She glanced down at the thin gold watch on her wrist, a present from Xie. Three a.m.

To an outside observer, she didn't look suspicious. Just a harmless, middle-aged Asian woman, probably visiting the building to clean the offices before the workers came in the next morning.

She removed her handbag from the car and pushed the door closed, then after one more glance toward the street, she turned and walked over to the warehouse door.

Glancing up at the camera over the door, she checked that the red light was off. She had disabled the camera remotely before coming, but again, she was a cautious woman.

Stepping closer, she entered a code into the keypad to the left of the door, and the door clicked open. She opened it wider, then slid through the gap and paused in the doorway, looking at the brightly lit shipping container in the middle of the floor. It had taken a while for her to set all this up, and it was a pity it was now going to waste.

She walked closer, quietly, her soft soled Hush Puppies making little noise on the concrete floor. Not that it would have made much difference to the young Chinese man sitting in front of the table, fast asleep, with his head cradled in his arms.

There was no sign of the other man. She had seen him leave earlier in the evening but had not monitored the security feed for sometime and had assumed he would already be back. She hesitated, pondering the consequences of him not being there, then decided it didn't matter.

Stepping closer, she dropped her handbag on the table, but when the sound still failed to wake the young man, she jabbed him in the shoulder with her finger.

He stirred, then looked up, blinking the sleep from his eyes. When he saw her, his eyes widened, and he jumped to his feet. His eyes darted toward the door as if looking for someone else, then looked back at her.

Clearing his throat, he said, "*Ni hao*. I was just..." he trailed off as he gestured toward the table.

"Where is the other one?"

"He's..." Again, his eyes darted toward the door. "He's gone to get some food. He... he said he was sick of noodles." Yu-Ming shrugged. "Of course I'm okay with noodles..."

"Change of plan," Mingmei interrupted him. "We're

moving the prisoner." She unzipped her handbag and removed a bundle of plastic zip-ties. "Secure her and bring her out."

He nodded eagerly, hurried to the shipping container, opened the door, and disappeared inside. Mingmei spotted a black hood lying on a chair and she walked over and picked it up.

"*Gankuai*," she called out. "Hurry up."

A short while later, the door widened, and the woman emerged, her hands tied behind her back. The young man nudged her forward, causing her to stumble.

Despite her ordeal and the late hour, the woman seemed remarkably composed. Her hair was only slightly disheveled, and Mingmei had to admit she was quite attractive for a Western woman.

The woman gazed silently at Mingmei, her brow lightly furrowed as if she were committing her face to memory.

"Put his on her." Mingmei tossed the hood over and the young man caught it in midair and pulled it over the woman's head.

"Good." Mingmei moved back to the table and picked up her handbag.

"Where are you taking me?" the woman asked, her voice muffled by the hood.

Mingmei walked over and looked up at her. The prisoner stood a good head taller than Mingmei and she had to tilt her head back.

"It doesn't matter," she replied calmly as she reached into her handbag. Withdrawing a SIG Sauer P365, she aimed it at the young man and pulled the trigger. The gunshot reverberated throughout the enclosed space, drowning out the scream from the hooded woman, who collapsed to her knees.

Mingmei flipped up the safety with her thumb, then slipped the SIG Sauer back into her handbag and looked down at the body of the young man. He had fallen onto his back, his eyes wide, a neat hole in the middle of his forehead. A pool of blood spread slowly from the back of his head.

It was a pity. He had been useful until now, but he was the only remaining link with China and had outlived his usefulness.

She turned back to the woman, who was silent but visibly shaking. She put a hand on her shoulder and the woman flinched.

"You will receive the same treatment if you don't cooperate. Do you understand?"

The woman's hooded head moved as she nodded.

"Good." Mingmei reached down and slipped her hand under the woman's arm and pulled her to her feet.

"Come on. Time to get moving."

49

Balancing paper bags filled with home-cooked food, Danny closed the car door with his hip and made his way toward the warehouse entrance. He had stayed out longer than intended. The prospect of a comfortable night in his own bed had been too attractive for Danny to turn down.

He was sure, though, that Yu-Ming would forgive him when he turned up with an armful of home-cooked food.

As he neared the entrance, he sensed something was off. It wasn't until he took a few more steps that he realized the door was slightly ajar.

Strange.

Glancing up at the camera, he noticed the red light was no longer blinking.

Very strange.

Shouldering the door open, he called out, "Yu-Ming. Why is the door open?"

There was no answer.

Stepping inside, he called out again. "Yu-Ming? Are you sleeping?"

He walked towards the tables and spotted Yu-Ming lying on the floor. Shaking his head, he remarked, "Man, you can sleep anywhere." Setting the bags down on the table, he approached him. "Wake up, dude. That floor must be freezing!"

It was then that he noticed the dark pool of liquid around Yu-Ming's head and the hole in his forehead.

"Miu Deus!" he exclaimed, coming to an abrupt halt, his mouth gaping open. His heart raced, and he swallowed back the contents of his stomach as they reappeared in his throat. "Yu-Ming," he called out, hoping against hope that his eyes were playing tricks on him, but there was no response.

"Shit, shit, shit, what do I do?" His hands shook and his legs felt unsteady beneath him. His head whipped around as he scanned the interior of the warehouse. Was the killer still there? His eyes fell upon the open door to the shipping container.

"Oh, no," he groaned. He took a deep breath and moved slowly toward the shipping container. "Please dear God, please." He reached the door, took a deep breath, and then peered inside. It was empty. He breathed a sigh of relief. He took another deep breath, then panic rose within him again. Where was she? How did she get out? He turned to look back at the body. Why did she shoot Yu-Ming? No, it can't have been her. She was too nice. Someone else must have done it. But who?

He stared at the body, his brain unable to function.

"Why? Why? Why?" His hands kept trembling as he leaned against the side of the shipping container for support. His breathing was shallow and rapid, and tears filled his eyes.

"What do I do? What do I do?" he kept repeating, unable to take his eyes off the body.

He had to get out of there. What if the police found him? The thought spurred him into action and he pushed himself away from the side of the container, carefully skirting the body, as if worried Yu-Ming would spring back to life. He moved toward the exit, slowly at first, then faster, before stopping suddenly midway. Had he left anything that might link him to the killing?

The only thing he had left was the food in the bags. Could that be traced back to his mum? He didn't know, but grabbed the bags just in case, then hurried back to the doorway. Setting the bags down on the floor, he slid his sleeve over his hand and opened the door, then gave the handle a wipe with his sleeve. He looked back over his shoulder. Perhaps he should wipe everything down?

The sound of an approaching vehicle in the road outside caught his attention, and he bent down and snatched the bags from the floor. He would have to take the risk. Hopefully, his prints would be mixed up in everyone else's.

Peering around the doorframe, he checked there was no-one outside, stepped out and hurried over to his car. Setting the bags on the roof of his Seat he unlocked the car then transferred them onto the passenger seat before looking back at the warehouse door. Should he close it?

Another vehicle passing in the street made the decision for him.

The best thing for him to do was to get far away from there.

Initially, Adriana attempted to keep count of the turns, hoping to distract herself from the shooting. However, after a while, she gave up. She hadn't known where they had started from and she quickly lost track of time, the journey seeming to take forever. She instead surrendered herself to the outcome and tried to make herself as comfortable as possible. Which wasn't easy, given the tight space she was crammed into.

After the gunshot, she had been led from the warehouse and pushed into the trunk of a small car. The hum of tires on the road surface eventually lulled her into an uneasy sleep and it was only when the road surface changed, a large bump sending shock waves through her body, that she became alert again.

The car rocked up and down as it traversed a rough surface, the engine note rising and falling, and stones ricocheted off the underside of the car.

After approximately five minutes, the car came to a halt, and she heard the front door open. She braced herself, waiting for the trunk lid to open, but nothing happened for a very long time. Feeling the aches and pains in her side and noticing her fingers going numb, she attempted to change position, but there wasn't enough room. She shifted her head against the trunk floor to loosen the rough hood, but it only tightened.

After a considerable amount of time had passed, she heard footsteps on gravel and then felt a rush of fresh cold air as the trunk was opened.

A hand grabbed her ankles and pulled them out into the open, then two hands grabbed hold of her shoulders and pulled her upright into a sitting position, her legs hanging over the lip of the trunk.

"Get out."

It was the Chinese woman's voice.

"How? I need help."

Hands pulled her forward, her legs lowering and finally her feet touching the ground. She stood and almost collapsed, her body disoriented from the hours of inactivity. A hand steadied her, and she slowly straightened up, grimacing as the blood flowed back into her limbs.

She took a deep breath, and despite the rough hessian cloth of the hood, the air felt fresher and cooler. Her surroundings seemed completely silent at first, but as she tuned in, she heard bird song and then the cry of a gull. There was a distinct scent of salt in the air.

She was near the ocean.

"This way."

She was tugged forward and felt soft gravel under her feet as she stumbled. After around twenty steps, she felt a hard surface underfoot.

"There's a step."

She gingerly tested the ground in front of her until she felt the step, then placed her weight on her foot and stepped

The Chinese Cat   173

forward. The surface changed again. It was still hard, but felt more pliant. A wooden floor, perhaps?

A floorboard creaked, confirming her guess.

A few steps later... "Stairs ahead of you. Climb them."

Adriana stopped. "No."

She heard a sigh, then felt something hard poke her in the small of her back.

"I can always shoot you."

Adriana gritted her teeth, then felt around in front of her with her toe until she felt the bottom of the stairs, then stepped forward.

She counted fifteen steps before the floor levelled out, then another five steps before she was pulled to a stop. She heard a door opening and then she was turned to her right and pushed forward. She stumbled, her footsteps audible on a bare wooden floor. When she stopped, she felt fingers gripping the hood and tugging it free from her head. Light assaulted her eyes, and she blinked furiously until they adjusted to the light, at the same time sucking in deep lungfuls of fresh air.

She felt movement around her hands and then heard a snip and her arms fell free beside her waist. Before she could turn around, she heard the door closing behind her and a heavy bolt sliding home.

Adriana shook her arms and wiggled her fingers as they tingled and jerked with pins and needles. She was in a bedroom, a single metal framed bed with a bare mattress pushed up against one wall. The ceiling was low and sloped unevenly toward an open window in the far wall. She walked over to the window and looked out. A rusted steel grill blocked her way in or out. She tried to tug it open, but it held firm, so she gave up and peered outside, trying to figure out her location. Facing east, she saw the sun still low in the sky, casting soft golden rays across open fields. There were no buildings for as far as she could see. Just fields. Some of them plowed, some dotted with cows and sheep. She focused her gaze closer, noticing a stone wall marking the edge of the field where it met the farmhouse, and below her window was a stone-flagged patio. Glancing to the right, she glimpsed the front of an older model blue Volkswagen parked on a patch of gravel, accompanied by a black van. Shifting her gaze to the left, she spotted an olive tree in a patch of dirt, with the stone wall continuing around it before wrapping back around the house.

Smelling cigarette smoke, she leaned forward and looked down at the area directly beneath her window.

There was a man dressed in black with an automatic weapon hanging from a sling. She watched him take a puff from his cigarette, then throw the butt on the ground and stub it out with a black boot. He walked away toward the olive tree and Adriana angled her head to watch him. As he turned the corner of the house, she caught a brief glimpse of his face.

He wasn't Chinese.

51

"No interruptions." Anson Liu growled into his phone, then set the receiver back on the cradle. Turning to his computer, he typed in a command, then watched as a video feed filled the screen. He tapped another key and sound came out from his computer speakers—muttered commands in Mandarin.

There was a tap on the door and, irritated, he looked up to see Wei in the doorway.

"Quick. They're going in now."

Wei stepped inside, closed the door behind him, and hurried over, taking up position just behind Anson's left shoulder, so he could see the screen.

The two men watched as the camera, a body-cam fitted to a man's load carrying vest, showed the interior of a van. Visible were three men, dressed in dark jeans and polo shirts, cloth masks covering the lower part of their faces. Two men were press checking their Glock 17s, while the third cradled a *Škorpion* VZ61 machine pistol.

The man wearing the body-cam counted down quietly, his fingers visible on screen, *"Wu, si, san, er, yi."* Then the side of the van slid open and without a word the men stepped out, the camera following them. They spread out, moving to some prearranged plan, weapons held at the ready.

Ahead of them was a dilapidated farmhouse, paint peeling from the woodwork, and weeds growing from the guttering. Two men split off to cover the left and right boundaries, disappearing from view, while the third man with the camera, and another advanced toward the front door. They positioned themselves on either side of the door, and one man, wearing gloves, tested the door handle. It turned, and the door creaked open, revealing a dim interior. The cameraman entered first, his weapon—a Glock—held steady as he scanned the room from right to left, then back again, following the other man's lead as he signaled to move into the next room. The two men split up, the camera now capturing a basic kitchen setup with pots and pans on a countertop beside a camping-style gas burner. Moving through to another door, the Glock swept left and then right as the man entered. The room was bare except for a wooden desk and chair, with a pen stand and a power strip still plugged in, a red light showing it was live. The camera panned across the room as the man searched, revealing colored pins and scraps of paper on the wall where documents had been removed. Exiting the room, the man rejoined the others in the living room, all of them shaking their heads. The cameraman's voice echoed from the speakers. "There's no one here, Sir."

"*Cào nǐ mā!*" Anson cursed, glanced at Wei, then leaned closer to the computer. "Check everything again, then burn the place to the ground."

He ended the feed without waiting for an answer, stabbing at his laptop with an angry finger. "The *sān bā,* the bitch, has gone."

He looked over at Wei, who was frowning back at him, waiting for instructions. "Why isn't she there?"

"That was the last known location of her phone, Sir, but it's been turned off for over nine hours now."

"So she could be anywhere by now?"

Wei nodded.

Anson put his fingertips to his brow and closed his eyes. She was a wily old hag, and he had been right not to trust her. He reached for his cell phone, scrolled through the phone book, then tapped on a number before putting the phone on speaker. He placed the phone down on the desk, then sat staring at it while it connected. It rang for a while before cutting out. He leaned forward and tapped redial. Both men stared at the phone as the phone rang out, and then once more went unanswered.

Anson cursed again, then swung around in his chair to look at Wei. "Track that phone. Find out where Zhang Yu-Ming is."

"Yes, sir." Wei nodded and moved toward the door.

"And when you get hold of him, find out where that *sān bā* has gone!"

52

Archie closed the manila folder, placed it on his lap, and prepared for landing by stowing his tray table.

He'd read through the file three times on the flight and memorized the contents.

John Hayes.

A very interesting man.

Archie had roused his faithful assistant at five in the morning to request a comprehensive report on John Hayes. Despite her grumbling, she had arranged for the file to be delivered to him in a sealed pouch just before his departure for Lisbon. While it would have been quicker to receive it via email, Archie preferred the feeling of paper between his fingers. He enjoyed seeing the words on a page rather than scrolling through an electronic device. He knew his colleagues made fun of him behind his back, but they couldn't argue with the results of his long career in the intelligence service.

He smiled at the pretty stewardess as she made her pre-landing checks and thought back to what he'd learnt about him. Hayes was an English citizen whose wife had tragically died in India, and who now resided in Lisbon. Despite no visible source of income, he held a significant stake in a Hong Kong property company called Pegasus Land. A shareholding that came shortly after the unusual death of the previous chairman of the company.[1]

But that was not the end of the strange events that occurred when John Hayes was around.

In Bangkok he had met Adriana D'Silva, an unknown journalist until she broke a story about the exploitation of refugees, causing a considerable scandal in Thai government circles.[2]

There was then a hostage event in Oman when John and Adriana were on holiday, where two dead bodies turned up in the desert. The bodies of the men who had held Adriana hostage.

Afterwards, Adriana's career soared, propelling her to minor celebrity status and earning her respect as a journalist.

John Hayes appeared in the news again when he was apprehended by the Turkish Army on the Syrian border, purportedly after rescuing a young Australian woman from ISIS. Archie still found this story difficult to believe.

Then there were Adriana's stories about sexual abuse and murder by Guru Atman in Sri Lanka, following John's visit to the ashram. He was the same guru who later died under mysterious circumstances in a fire at his ashram in India.

Archie glanced out the window as the plane descended during its final approach, passing through clusters of fluffy white cumulus clouds. Although John Hayes had never been implicated in the deaths that appeared to trail him, it felt like an extraordinarily strange series of events. And that was before the incident involving Xie Longwei was thrown into the mix.

Archie was very interested in meeting him. There was nothing like looking a man in the eye when you asked him a question, something his colleagues failed to understand. On the phone, you would hear an answer, but communication was so much more than that. It was all about the subtleties of body language, the tone of voice, and the movement of the eyes.

Thirty minutes later, Archie had cleared immigration without a hitch, the benefits of being seated in the front row and traveling on a diplomatic passport.

He walked outside the airport and nodded at the uniformed driver holding a sign that said 'Cholmondeley-Warner.'

"*Bom dia*, Sir." The driver beamed a greeting, then he looked past him and his smile faded. "No luggage, Sir?"

"No." Archie winked. "Just me."

The driver nodded and led the way over to a black S Class Mercedes parked at the curb and opened the rear door. Archie slid inside and waited for the driver to climb in. The driver looked up into the rear-view mirror. "Straight to the hotel, Sir?"

"Yes, quick as you can, old chap."

---

1. See "A million Reasons: John Hayes #2"
2. See "A New Beginning: John Hayes #3"

53

John stumbled out of the bedroom as the smell of frying bacon filled the air.

"Why didn't you wake me? Look at the time."

Steve glanced back over his shoulder, then turned his attention back to the frying pan. "Mate, you needed the rest. And there's nothing we can do right now until we come up with a good plan."

John rubbed his face and ran his fingers through his hair. He was loath to admit it, but Steve was right. He sat down at the breakfast bar as Steve loaded two plates with bacon and eggs.

John noticed a full French press on the countertop, so he reached over, grabbed it, and filled the empty mug in front of him.

"I made it just the way you taught me." Steve winked as he carried the two plates of food over and set them down.

John took a sip, nodded his approval, then set the mug down and picked up his knife and fork. His stomach growled loudly. He hadn't eaten properly since the previous morning, barely touching the takeout Steve had arranged the night before.

He sliced a rasher of bacon and speared it with his fork, pausing with the fork halfway to his mouth. "Thanks, Steve. You're a good friend."

Steve shrugged and made in-roads into his own breakfast.

"Anything from Ramesh?"

Steve shook his head and spoke through a mouthful of bacon. "Nothing yet, mate."

John grimaced and shook his head, wondering if there was any way they could gain an advantage. Absentmindedly, he mopped up some egg yolk with a rasher of bacon and popped it into his mouth, but then a pang of guilt hit him, halting his chewing. He wondered what Adriana was eating at that moment, if she had slept, and if her captors were taking care of her.

As if sensing his thoughts, Steve glanced over and remarked, "Skipping meals won't help her. And neither will skipping sleep. We need to stay sharp, mate."

"Yeah," John mumbled and began chewing again.

The two men finished their breakfast in silence, punctuating mouthfuls of bacon and egg with sips of coffee, and by the time John had finished and pushed his plate away, he was feeling ready to take on the day again.

Steve was right. Yesterday had taken a lot out of him—emotionally and physically—and he hadn't realized how exhausted he was until his head hit the pillow. Even then it had taken a long time for him to actually sleep, his body sore and his brain working overtime, tossing and turning until finally, in the small hours, exhaustion won the battle.

He leaned back in his chair and crossed his arms, staring down at his empty plate.

The task ahead was enormous, and if he looked at it in its entirety, it was overwhelming. He needed to break it down, as he always did, into little steps, and just focus on the next one.

He looked up at Steve, who was wiping his mouth with the back of his hand.

"I do have napkins, you know," John remarked.

Steve grinned. "I couldn't find them."

"Did you look?" John grinned back. He stood and reached for the French press. "I'll brew some more coffee. We have a lot of planning to do."

John walked around the breakfast bar and into the kitchen as Steve gathered the plates.

Just then, John's phone began buzzing. He set the French press down and hurried to the bedroom where it was charging. Picking up his phone, he glanced at the screen. It displayed a UK number he hadn't seen before. Carrying the phone back to the kitchen, he looked at Steve.

"Unknown number," he said, tapping the screen before putting the phone on speaker.

"Hello?"

"John Hayes?"

"Yes."

"My name is Archibold Cholmondeley-Warner. I'm with the Ministry of Foreign Affairs."

John frowned. The voice was deep, confident, and spoke with an upper-class English accent.

"I understand your... companion... a Ms. Adriana D'Silva, has gone missing."

John frowned deeper and looked up at Steve. Steve had come out of the kitchen and was wiping his hands on a dishcloth.

"How did you get my number?" John asked.

"From the Winchester Police."

"Okay."

"I wondered if perhaps we could meet, Mr. Hayes."

John was shaking his head. "I'm sorry I'm not in the UK right now. So that won't be possible."

"I know that, Mr. Hayes. I'm here in Lisbon... as are you."

John frowned at Steve, whose expression matched his own.

"Who did you say you were again?"

"Archibold Cholmondeley-Warner of the Ministry of Foreign Affairs."

"And why do you want to speak to me?"

John heard the man take a breath. "Mr. Hayes, a foreign national, has been kidnapped on British soil and transported out of the country by private plane. This is a very serious matter. I would like to get some background on the events and try to understand what is happening."

John muted the call and looked up at Steve. "How does he know so much?"

Steve shrugged. "The cop must have told him everything."

John nodded. Perhaps he was right. Perhaps he was being overly suspicious. But he didn't want to waste time speaking to government servants. He tapped the phone again.

"Mr. Cholmondeley-Warner, I'm sorry, but I can't tell you anything the Winchester Police won't have already told you. I suggest if you have any questions, you speak to them again."

"Mr. Hayes, in my experience, it's always good to get multiple sides of a story. Everyone will have a different understanding of events, and somewhere in between each version is the truth. Why don't you come and meet me today at my hotel? I'm at the Pestana Palace. Join me for lunch."

"Look, I appreciate the invitation, but I don't see how I can help you. I understand the police are doing everything they can and, to be quite honest, the last thing on my mind right now is having lunch with someone I've never met."

"Hmmmm, okay. But what if I said to you I believe this is all connected to a Mr. Xie Longwei who disappeared a year ago just up the road from where Ms. D'Silva was taken?"

John stared at the phone in shock. Fuck! Who was this guy? He stared at Steve while thinking about what to say.

Steve pointed at his chest, then made a talking sign with his hand before holding his finger to his lips.

John nodded, put the call on mute again, and asked, "Who the hell is this guy?"

Steve shrugged. "If he was a cop, he would say so. But I don't think he's just a government official. My guess is British intelligence."

"MI6?" John's eyes widened.

"Could be."

"Shit."

"Mr. Hayes?" Archibold's voice rang out from the phone speaker. John ignored it, his mind racing. How much did they know? What were the consequences? Would Adriana be saved only for him to be thrown in prison for Xie's disappearance?

"I think you should meet him." Steve added. "You never know what will come of it. Anyway, we don't have a plan yet."

"Mr. Hayes? Are you still there?"

John unmuted the call. "You're not really with Foreign Affairs, are you?"

Archibold chuckled. "Why on earth would you think

that?" He chuckled again. "Join me for lunch and we'll try to get to the bottom of this whole matter."

John looked up at Steve, who nodded.

"Okay."

"Good. One o'clock at the Bar Allegro? We'll get acquainted and then have something to eat."

John ended the call and again looked at Steve, more confused than ever.

54

Danny had been driving for hours without stopping. Initially, he had driven around in a panic, haunted by the image of Yu-Ming's lifeless body. He had anxiously checked his mirrors, half-expecting to see police lights or Yu-Ming's assailant at any moment. Eventually, he calmed down enough to think rationally. He had watched enough crime movies to know he should take a random route, making regular turns and changes of direction, to confuse anyone who might be following. However, as the fuel gauge neared empty, he was forced to pull over at a gas station to refill the tank. Though he was fairly certain no one was tailing him at this point, he still stood nervously scanning the road while waiting for the tank to fill up.

Once the tank was full, he went inside to pay the cashier and noticed a rack of burner phones.

"Damn it," he muttered aloud, earning a disapproving look from the cashier. Ignoring her, he retrieved his phone from his pocket and stared at it.

All his evasive driving over the last few hours had been a waste of time. They were probably tracking his phone. He turned it off and attempted to remove the SIM card, but then realized he didn't have a pin to insert in the hole.

"Shit," he cursed again, but he grabbed a burner phone from the rack and approached the cashier.

"Is something wrong?"

"No, no," Danny answered hurriedly, as he handed over the cash. "I forgot an appointment," he added, keeping his head turned away from the camera he had just noticed above the cashier's head. Taking the change, he hurried back to his car, hoping he hadn't made himself too memorable.

Five minutes later, he parked in a quiet lane and retrieved his phone from the passenger seat. He knew he had to get rid of it, but it hurt him. It was a relatively new iPhone, and had cost him a sizeable chunk of his meagre savings. But it was the phone or prison. He rummaged through the clutter of receipts and other debris in the cup holders between the seats until he unearthed an old toothpick, its tip still encrusted with dried-up food.

He used it to pop the SIM from the phone, then snapped the SIM in two and tossed it and the toothpick out of the window. He again looked at the phone. Maybe he could still keep it? But then the image of Yu-Ming flashed before his eyes and he decided against it. He tossed the phone out the window too, then unboxed the burner. He sat staring out the windshield while he waited for the phone to power up.

What should he do now? He couldn't go home. Whoever killed Yu-Ming might be waiting for him there. The cops too.

The phone screen flashed as it powered on, and he dialed a number from memory and waited.

"Mum, it's me, Danny. I lost my phone this morning, so this is my new number… yes yes, I know… I should be more careful... listen Mum, I'm working some extra shifts so I won't be home for a while... yes, I'll eat properly... I don't know, Mum... I'll call you... bye, bye... yes, me too."

He ended the call, tossed the phone on the seat beside him, and rubbed his face. The adrenaline from earlier had all but left his body and despite the full night's sleep in his own bed, he suddenly felt exhausted. His eyes closed, and he slumped down in his seat, a wave of fatigue washing over him. But with his eyes closed, all he could see was Yu-Ming's cold, lifeless eyes looking back at him.

Danny wished he'd never taken up the job. He now had nowhere to go, no-one to speak to, no-one to ask for help. His shoulders shook and he let out a sob of frustration and despair. What should he do? The sob became another, and another, until tears streamed down his face and his body shook with grief.

55

John was about to leave the apartment for his lunch meeting when the intercom buzzed. He walked over and picked up the receiver.

"*Senhor* Hayes?"

"Yes, Miguel."

"The man you asked about? The one who gave me the cat."

John frowned. "What about him?"

"Well, *Senhor*, he's sitting in the café across the street."

"What?" John spun around and snapped his fingers to get Steve's attention. "Are you sure?"

"*Sim, Senhor*. At first I wasn't sure. You know these Chinese they all look the same, but I've been watching him for the last fifteen minutes and I'm sure it's him."

"Okay, Miguel. Where's he sitting and what's he wearing?"

"He's at a table on the right-hand side. Jeans and a hoodie, but... he's the only Chinese man in there, so he's easy to see."

"Right-hand side, jeans and hoodie, Chinese," John

repeated while gesturing at Steve to move to the window overlooking the street.

Steve hurried over and looked out, then signaled with a thumbs up.

"Thank you, Miguel. I appreciate it," John said and replaced the receiver back in its cradle.

"He's our guy," he growled at Steve as he joined him at the window, spotting the Chinese man immediately. "He's the guy who left the *Jiu Choi Maau* in the lobby."

"What should we do?"

John chewed his lip while he glared down at the man just visible in the café's window. He could be their only connection to Adriana.

"We need to speak to him." John thought for a moment, then, without taking his eyes off the street, he added, "Bring him up here. I'm assuming he knows what I look like and he'll scarper as soon as I cross the street. But he doesn't know you."

"Do you think he'll come?"

"Don't give him a choice. You're almost twice his size. I'm sure you can persuade him."

"Righto. Back in a minute."

John kept his eyes on the man, reluctant to lose sight of him even for a second, and waited for Steve to come into view.

Steve didn't appear in the street for a while and John was wondering what was taking him so long when he saw Steve walking along the footpath on the same side of the café. John nodded approval. His friend must have exited the building and then, rather than walking straight across to the café, had gone down the street before crossing the road. John leaned forward, his nose almost touching the glass, and held his breath, willing Steve to get to the man before he suspected something. He watched as the big Australian entered the café and disappeared, then saw the Chinese man jerked back from the window.

Then nothing happened for what seemed like an eternity.

"Come on, Steve," John muttered, finally exhaling with relief as he saw the Chinese man exit the café with Steve very close behind him. As they turned toward John's building, he could see Steve had a firm grip on the man's elbow and was propelling him across the street.

John rushed to the intercom and dialed the lobby.

"Miguel, let those two men in immediately."

"*Sim, Senhor* Hayes."

John ended the call and opened the door. He walked into the corridor and watched the numbers above the elevators. The one on the left began moving, and he waited nervously as the numbers climbed until, with a ping, the elevator reached his floor and the doors slid open.

The Chinese man exited first, and he froze when he saw John.

He was younger than John expected, perhaps in his early twenties. He looked tired and drawn, and his eyes darted nervously as he licked his lips.

Steve gave him a shove in the back, pushing the man toward John. "He speaks English."

John stood to one side, and gestured toward his apartment door. "I think we need to have a conversation."

56

John stared at the young man seated in front of him. Steve loomed behind him, arms crossed and legs spread apart, but the young man showed no signs of attempting to escape. His shoulders drooped, and he stared blankly at the floor between himself and John.

"What's your name?"

The man's eyes darted to John, then back to the floor.

John took a deep breath and looked up at Steve. Steve shrugged.

John grabbed another chair from next to the dining table, set it down in front of the young man, and sat down.

"A couple of days ago, you left a cat in our lobby. A *Jiu Choi Maau.*"

Surprise flashed across the young man's face.

"Yes, I know it was you. What I don't know is why?"

The man swallowed but stayed silent.

There was nothing to connect this man with Adriana's kidnapping apart from a waving cat ornament, but John's gut told him he was involved.

Leaning forward with his elbows on his knees, John

lowered his head until the young man couldn't evade his gaze. "Where is she?" he demanded.

The man's eyes darted in panic, and he squirmed in his chair, as if searching for an escape route. Steve's large, calloused hand clamped down on his shoulder, holding him in place.

John gestured for Steve to step back, but maintained eye contact with the young man.

"We're not going to hurt you," he said in a low voice. "All we want to know is where she is."

The man gulped and shook his head. "I don't know."

John ground his teeth together, struggling to contain his frustration.

"Have you seen her?"

The man nodded.

John fought the urge to leap forward. "Where?"

The man swallowed again and looked up. "Abrunheira."

"Abrunheira?"

The man nodded.

"You know it?" Steve asked.

John nodded.

"Where in Abrunheira? Can you take me there?" he asked.

The man nodded. "But... she's not there now."

"Fuck!" John cursed and thumped his thigh. "Where the fuck is she, then?"

"I don't know," the young man said, shaking his head, and then began to cry.

John buried his face in his hands. Was he ever going to get a break? He massaged his eye sockets with his fingertips, then sat up straight.

"Steve, can you make us some coffee? I think we're going to need it."

Steve nodded and walked into the kitchen.

John reached out and put a hand on the young man's knee. "Let's start again. What's your name?"

The young man sniffed, wiped his face with the back of his hand, and said, "Danny."

"Okay, Danny, my name is John."

Danny nodded.

"Tell me, when was the last time you saw her?"

"Yesterday, when... I took her some food."

"In Abrunheira?"

"Yes." Danny sat up straighter. "I was guard... watching her. Me and ..." he trailed off.

"You and who?"

"Yu-Ming... he was from China." A tear ran down his cheek. "He's dead now."

John shot a glance in Steve's direction to make sure he was hearing the conversation, then leaned forward. "Dead?"

Danny nodded. "I went back this morning with some food. He... was lying on the floor..." A sob escaped his lips. "There was a hole in his head."

"He'd been shot?"

Danny nodded.

"And the woman?"

"Gone."

John clenched his jaw, and his hands tightened into fists. He paused and took a deep breath, but before he could say anything, Danny spoke again.

"We've been watching you for months." He swivelled in his chair and looked towards the window. "From across the street there."

He stood and Steve moved quickly across the kitchen as if to stop him, but John held up his hand. He followed Danny over to the window.

The young man pointed at a window diagonally opposite John's building. "From there. Me and Yu-Ming. We had a camera and a parabolic microphone."

John frowned at the building, but waited for Danny to continue.

"Every day I had to send a report and photos. What time you got up. What time you went to bed. What you did all day. Where you went." He turned to look at John with wide eyes. "I didn't know they were going to take her, I swear."

John nodded. He glanced back at the building. "Is there anyone there now?"

Danny shook his head. "I don't think so. It was just me and Yu-Ming. There were others in the beginning, but they got called back to China."

"So then, what happened in Abrunheira?"

Danny took a deep breath and turned away from the window. He watched as Steve walked over with two steaming mugs of coffee. John took one and nodded to Danny to take the other.

He held it in his hand and stared at the steam spiraling off the top. "We were told to report to an address in Abrunheira. A warehouse. When we got there, they told us we had to look after a prisoner." He looked up at John. "I didn't know it was her at first. But when the other men left, I had to take some food for her and then I recognized her... from here."

"Was she hurt?"

Danny shook his head. "No. She was okay." He stared across the room as he remembered. "She spoke to me. She told me her name. Adriana D'Silva. Told me to google her." He looked back at John. "All this time I had no idea who we were watching... I... I didn't care. I mean, I'm not a bad guy.

When they asked me, I didn't have a job. It was easy money. I swear I didn't know anyone was going to get hurt."

John gestured toward the chair. "Come sit down." He nodded at the untouched coffee mug in Danny's hand. "Drink your coffee."

John waited until Danny had sat back in front of him, then he looked over at Steve, who stood with his butt against the kitchen countertop, sipping his coffee.

"Get our friend on the line. I want him to hear all of this."

Turning back to Danny, he said. "Now I want to hear everything. Right from the beginning."

57

Archie finished his martini and turned his wrist to look at the time. John Hayes was forty-five minutes late.

In other words, he wasn't coming.

Archie dabbed his mouth with a white cloth napkin, nodded a thank you to the barman and slid off the bar stool. He retrieved his phone from the inside pocket of his suit jacket and looked around the bar. There were only a couple of tables occupied and no-one nearby.

He moved over to a vacant table, away from the bar, and out of earshot of the other customers, scrolled through his phone book, selected a number and dialed.

Archie waited as the phone rang and was about to give up when the call was answered.

"I hope this is a courtesy call," a deep voice growled in perfect, accent-less English.

"Lovely to hear your voice, too," Archie quipped.

"I'm sure. And to what do I owe the pleasure?"

"I need a favor."

"Ha!" the man on the other end of the line scoffed. "Don't you always?"

"And I always repay them, Francisco."

"That you do, my friend. That you do."

Archie heard Francisco take a deep breath and rustle some paper.

"So, what do you need this time?"

"I need you to track a number for me."

"Are you running something on my turf?"

Archie chuckled. "Nothing like that, old chap. I'm just concerned about the whereabouts of one of my citizens... who just happens to be in Lisbon."

"I see." There was a long pause. "And where are you?"

"I'll be waiting for your call, Francisco."

"At the Pestana, as usual, I'm sure."

Archie chuckled. "There's a reason you're in the job you are. Why don't you come and join me for a drink? Not today, I'm a little busy. But I'll let you know when I'm free."

"Hmmm. Don't go causing any trouble. Send me the number and I'll look into it."

"Thank you, my friend."

Archie ended the call, shared John Hayes' number, then checked his watch again. Maybe he would have time for a quick bite to eat? Nothing too big. Because he knew it wouldn't take long for Francisco Almeida e Cunha, Director of the *Serviço de Informações de Segurança*, the Portuguese Secret Service, to get back to him.

58

Joseph waited patiently beside the window overlooking the perfectly manicured lawns of the Presidential Palace. Behind him, he could hear the clicking of keys as the President's secretary typed away on her keyboard.

He was content to wait. Even though he was the Minister of Defense and the President was his father, he never let that get in the way of protocol and procedure. He waited his turn, just like everyone else.

He had barely slept the night before, a million thoughts fighting for supremacy inside his head. Giving up at four a.m., he got dressed and drove to the barracks of the NSOR —the Nkuru Special Operations Regiment—for an unexpected visit. Joseph took pride in maintaining a high level of combat fitness and frequently trained with the regiment, where he had served before becoming Defense Minister.

Showered and changed, he now experienced that familiar satisfaction that followed a rigorous workout. Most importantly, his mind was focused on the task ahead: convincing his father.

"You can go in now, Sir."

Joseph turned to the beautiful young woman behind the desk and offered a smile. She returned it, holding his gaze for longer than expected. She was Mbanu, a tribe known for their striking appearance—tall, slim, with expressive dark eyes and smooth ebony skin. However, Joseph never mixed work with pleasure. A man was nothing if he didn't stand by his principles.

He tapped on the double height mahogany door, then without waiting for an answer, opened it and stepped inside.

His father sat behind a large teak desk, his back to a massive arched window with a view over the Presidential lawns. He glanced up as Joseph walked in, smiled, gestured towards a leather chair, and then returned his attention to the document on his desk.

Joseph sat and observed his father as he went about his work. Despite being in his early sixties, his father remained as agile and energetic as he had been two decades ago. His hair was closely cropped, its gray hue standing out against his otherwise rich chocolate brown complexion. His face bore few wrinkles, and aside from his hair color, the only other sign of his age was the pair of gold-rimmed reading glasses resting on the bridge of his nose.

Finally, with a flourish of an expensive-looking fountain pen, he signed the document and set it to one side before removing his glasses and sitting back in his chair, smiling warmly.

"Good morning, son." His eyes twinkled with pleasure.

Joseph was the only child born from his father's early, unsuccessful marriage. President Babatunde Tamba harbored certain sexual preferences, a closely guarded secret within Nkuru's intensely masculine society, and had remained single ever since. However, regardless of his private life, he remained fiercely loyal to his country's citizens, dedicating all his actions to their welfare. Moreover, he cherished his son deeply, and Joseph made every effort to ensure his father's continual pride in him.

"Father."

"Can I get you something to drink? Some *attaya?*"

Joseph smiled and shook his head. He'd had breakfast much earlier and *attaya*, the popular sweetened tea, was too sweet for his tastes.

"Coffee?" his father insisted.

Joseph grinned and gave in. "I'll take a coffee, please."

Babatunde nodded approval and pressed a button on his phone. "Aminata, please bring some coffee for my son. Thank you."

"Nothing for you, father?" Joseph asked.

Babatunde shook his head. "No, I'm doing this new thing. Intermittent fasting. I don't eat anything until lunchtime. It's very popular in Western countries, you know." He ran his hand down over his stomach. "I have to keep myself trim."

Joseph chuckled. "Are you getting vain in your old age?"

Babatunde grinned indulgently. "Wait until you're my age, son. It's not so easy to keep in shape." He sighed. "But jokes aside, there are health benefits too. I need to keep in good health if I'm to lead this country properly."

Joseph blinked. His father had been talking a lot about health recently. Was he hiding something? He made a mental note to make some discreet enquiries with the Palace physician.

They continued with small talk for a few more minutes until Aminata arrived with the coffee.

Joseph stared out the window as she poured the coffee, avoiding eye contact, and waited until she left the room, the door closing behind her before sitting forward and picking up the coffee cup.

"She likes you, son."

Joseph held the cup to his lips, then paused. "Have you forgotten the expression 'don't dirty your own compound', Father?"

His father nodded ruefully. "You're right, son. That's something I learnt the hard way."

Joseph sipped his coffee to avoid saying more. The Chinese Communist Party had only got their foot in the door because of his father 'dirtying his compound' and both knew it was something he would never do again.

"Anyway, much as I love to see my son, I know you well enough to know something is troubling you."

Joseph slowly set his cup down, composing his thoughts. He sat back in his chair and crossed one leg over the other. When he looked up, he could see his father studying him with concern.

"It's about our special guest."

Babatunde nodded slowly. "The one that doesn't exist."

"The one that doesn't exist," Joseph repeated. "Unfortunately, we have a problem."

59

"You never explained why you were hanging around outside my building?" John's eyes met Danny's in the rear-view mirror as he spoke.

The young Chinese man sat in the middle of the rear seat, his arms crossed, looking unhappily between the gap in the front seats.

He swallowed and averted his gaze.

John turned his attention back to the road and jammed his foot on the brake as a taxi pulled out from a side street without looking.

"Idiot," Steve muttered from the seat beside John.

John shrugged and looked back in the rear-view mirror. "Well?"

Danny sniffed. "Once I saw what they did to Yu-Ming... I had nowhere else to go."

"But why my place? You've been spying on us for months. How do you know we're not involved?"

"Because I stopped believing I was on the right side. *Senhora* D'Silva... I saw her work... she's not a bad person... so I guessed you weren't either. I couldn't go home. I can't go to the police. So I came to your building, hoping maybe something would happen. Something to help me."

John nodded, thinking it over. It sounded plausible. Much more plausible than the rest of his story. He ran his mind back over everything Danny had told him in the last couple of hours. Months of surveillance, tattooed mercenaries, Adriana in a shipping container, and a tenuous connection to the Chinese Government. It all sounded like a badly written Netflix series.

He compared it to what he knew as fact. The kidnappers were Chinese. The ransom demand was 'Xie for Adriana'.

Someone was spending a lot of money on this operation. His intuition pointed toward the woman orchestrating everything, but did she also have support from the CCP? Why employ Danny if they were involved? And then why were the government operatives called back to China?

Who killed Yu-Ming? Was someone else involved?

Nothing made sense and the more he thought about it, the more frustrated he got.

"Take the next left." Danny spoke from the rear and John slowed and indicated left.

He pulled into a narrower street lined with older brick and concrete commercial buildings in various states of disrepair.

"A thriving area," Steve muttered sarcastically.

"Which building?" John asked as he slowed to a crawl.

Danny pointed. "The third one up there on the right."

John rolled slowly past and scanned the front of the building and then the parking lot in front of the warehouse door. It was empty and there were no signs of life. John turned left at the end of the street, drove on a little way, then pulled the rented BMW X5 to the curb and stopped. He turned in his seat and looked at Steve.

"What do you think?"

Steve shrugged. "Looked empty to me, and no cops. No crime scene tape to suggest they have been there, either."

"Hmmm." John looked back at Danny. The young man seemed uncomfortable. Was it all a trap?

John wrinkled his face and stared out through the windshield. He had to get a look inside the warehouse.

"Right, Steve, take the wheel. I need to see inside." John retrieved his earbuds from the coin tray and inserted them in his ears. He then dialed Steve's number and said, "keep the line open. Park at the end of the street and let me know if anyone's coming."

"Yup."

John unfastened his seat belt and climbed out of the car. While Steve took his place behind the wheel, John opened the rear door and reached inside for Danny's arm. "You're coming with me."

60

Danny pulled his hoodie over his head, buried his hands in his pockets, and walked reluctantly toward the warehouse. John followed two paces behind, his eyes scanning the street and the surrounding buildings, looking for any signs of danger.

He heard a car engine and glanced back over his shoulder to see the black X5 pulling into the street and parking at the curb.

"I can see you," Steve's voice sounded in his earbud.

"Copy. Keep your eyes peeled," John replied.

They arrived at the open gate to the parking lot next to the warehouse, and Danny hesitated.

John halted behind him, surveying the building. "Do you notice anything unusual?"

Danny studied the warehouse. "No."

"How do we get in?"

Danny nodded toward the loading door. "Over there."

"Go on then."

Danny led the way across the parking lot and down the side of the building before stopping beside an access door next to the loading bay. He pointed at the security camera above the door. "It's turned off."

"Ok," John nodded at the keypad beside the door. "What about this?"

Danny stepped forward and, ignoring the keypad, pushed on the door. It swung open with a groan, revealing the dark warehouse interior.

Danny paused, waiting for instructions.

"Wait." John held up his hand. "Steve, all clear?"

"Not a dicky bird, mate."

John nodded and motioned for Danny to enter the building. After Danny went in, John leaned forward to peer inside. With some light filtering through high-set windows, he could just make out the interior, which seemed deserted.

He joined Danny inside and stood beside him. Danny was gazing at a spot across the building. "He's not there."

"Who?"

"Yu-Ming. His body was..." Danny pointed.

There was a single shipping container in the centre of the room with its doors slightly ajar. Beside it was a stack of cardboard boxes and several slabs of packaged drinking water. There were a couple of trestle tables and plastic chairs, but nothing else.

John approached the shipping container with his heart pounding. Despite Danny's assurance that she wasn't there, this was his only lead to Adriana. He cautiously extended his hand to open the door wider. The hinges squeaked loudly. It was dark inside, so John pulled out his cell phone and, using the flashlight, illuminated the interior.

In the corner, he spotted a mattress, along with several empty water bottles, scattered on the floor. Near the door, a plastic bucket emitted a strong odor of urine.

"Bastards," he cursed, his grip on his phone tightening.

He sensed Danny behind him, and it was all he could do to prevent himself from lashing out and punching the young man in the face. Gaining control, he stepped inside and walked slowly toward the mattress and crouched down. The sheet covering the mattress and the pillow case were a matching set from a child's bed. Thomas the Tank Engine motifs covered the sheet and the pillow, and a plain army blanket was crumpled at the foot of the bed. He reached out, his fingers touching the pillow as if by doing so he could connect with Adriana.

But there was nothing.

He lifted the pillow, hoping to catch a hint of her scent, but all he detected was the artificial floral aroma of detergent. Disappointed, he stood up and exited the container, scowling at Danny as he passed.

61

"She was here, Steve."

"So he wasn't lying."

John glanced at Danny standing in front of the shipping container, his hands thrust deep in his pockets again, staring morosely at the floor.

"No. Everything is as he said it would be. Apart from the body."

"Weird."

"Yeah," John sighed. "And we're still no closer to finding her."

"We'll find her, John, I know we will. Shall I come and pick you up?"

"Give me a couple more minutes. I want to look around."

"Copy."

John walked over to Danny and looked down at the floor.

"He was here. I saw him." Danny looked up. "I'm not lying."

"I believe you." John crouched down and turned on the phone flashlight and examined the floor. He moved his head and the flashlight, examining the concrete from different angles. "See this here." He pointed at a section of the floor. "See how the color changes? This section here is cleaner than the rest." He looked up at Danny. "You said there was blood?"

Danny nodded.

"Someone cleaned it up." He knelt down, leaned close to the floor, and sniffed. "I can smell chemicals. Like bleach." He pushed himself up and stood up. "Someone took the body away and then cleaned it all up."

"It's not the police," said Steve's voice in his ear. "A crime scene wouldn't be sanitized so quickly."

"I agree, Steve." John turned to face Danny. "Who do you think it was, Danny?"

Danny shook his head. "I've no idea. I really don't."

"You can't think of anyone?"

"No," Danny shook his head vigorously. "It's just been Yu-Ming and me for months. The only other people we met were the guys in black. The tattooed ones. And why would they kill him? They could have killed us when they met us."

John stared at Danny, but couldn't think of anything else to ask. He turned and looked around, checking to see if he had missed anything, but there was nothing else useful.

"Steve, you can pick us up."

"Wait one, there's a car coming."

John frowned, his heart rate immediately doubling. He grabbed Danny's arm and began walking toward the door.

"What's happening, Steve?"

"Green Jaguar SUV. Single male occupant. Looks okay, but heading your way. Wait."

John reached the door and pushed Danny up against the wall, and held his finger to his lips.

"He's slowing... he's stopped by the entrance... fuck, wait, he's getting out..."

"Cop? Chinese?"

Danny's eyes widened in panic, and John motioned for him to stay calm.

"No... middle-aged male... suit... skinny bugger... looks like a businessman to me," Steve continued.

"What's he doing?"

"Standing beside the car, looking around... maybe he's a real estate agent? Oh shit, he's entering the compound."

John thought fast. He couldn't afford for anyone to find him inside the property. Easing the door shut, he leaned back against it. He once again warned Danny to be quiet. "Someone's coming. Probably a real estate agent."

Danny stared back, his eyes wide with fear, but he didn't move.

"Steve, where is he?" John whispered.

"I've lost sight of him... two secs, I'll drive by."

John heard the rumble of the BMW's six-cylinder engine as Steve started the car. He waited, picturing the street in his head, calculating when Steve would reach the building. His calculations were a little fast, because it took slightly longer for Steve's voice to come online.

"He's standing in front of the loading door..."

"Doing what?" John hissed in reply.

"Looking... no wait, he's walking toward the door."

John tensed and leaned with all his weight against the door. He heard footsteps, the click click of steel heel taps, and then they stopped.

There was a knock on the door and a simultaneous loud intake of breath from Danny.

John glared at him and waited. The door handle wiggled and John held his breath.

"I can't see him anymore, John," said Steve in his ear. "I'm coming in."

Before John could even think of a reply, he heard a plummy English voice. One he'd heard before.

"Mr. Hayes. I know you're in there. I think we need to talk."

62

John and Steve leaned up against the wall, watching Archibold Cholmondeley-Warner wander around the warehouse.

Danny crouched beside them in a full squat, paying no attention to any of the men, lost in his own thoughts.

"He's definitely a spook." Steve muttered from the corner of his mouth. "Posh, public school education, knows everything about you..."

John narrowed his eyes, but remained silent. His mind raced as he considered this new development and how he could use it to his advantage. He didn't care who anyone worked for as long as he got Adriana back.

Archibold wandered slowly back toward them, the steel heel caps on his brogues clicking across the concrete floor like a tap dancer. Stopping in front of the two men, he looked down at the floor and nodded slowly at some unspoken thought.

Suddenly, he looked up and with a smile said, "Right. I

think I've seen enough. Let's go back to my hotel and see what we can do about it."

John exchanged a look with Steve.

"Ah... why would we do that?" he asked.

Archibold's smile broadened. "I've learnt a bit about you, Mr. Hayes. You're a resourceful man, and you will not rest until this matter is resolved. I believe I can help you."

"And why would you do that? Mr. Cholmondeley-Warner of the Ministry of Foreign Affairs."

Archibold chuckled and adjusted the lapel of his suit jacket. When he looked up, though, his expression was serious. "I believe we're dealing with a rogue element of the *Guojia Anquan Bu*. Do you know who they are?"

John nodded.

"I thought you might. Well, let's just say the opportunity to get one over on them is not something I like to miss." He shrugged and grinned again. "And Ms. D'Silva is a Portuguese citizen. Rescuing her from the clutches of the Chinese will gain me significant merit with my counterparts here in Portugal. Another opportunity I won't turn down."

"Huh. I told you he was a spook."

Archibold winked at Steve.

John studied Archibold's face, still frowning, then shrugged. "Ok, I'll listen to what you have to say."

"Excellent. Why don't you ride with me?" He turned and grinned at Steve. "Why don't you bring the young Chinese man and follow me in the black BMW you were sitting in earlier?"

63

John watched the streets go by as Archibold piloted the Jaguar with skill and confidence through the narrow cobble-stoned streets.

"You've been here before." It wasn't a question.

Archibold nodded. "Once or twice." He glanced over at John. "Some of our less savory countrymen like to make the city home."

John grunted.

"I'm not including you in that statement, of course, Mr. Hayes... can I call you John?"

"If I can call you Archibold. Your name is rather a mouthful."

"Please, call me Archie. All my friends do."

"Am I a friend?" John asked with raised eyebrows.

"That's up to you." Archie took his eyes off the road and took a long look at John. "We're on the same side, John."

John shrugged. "If you say so. But I judge a man by his deeds, and I've only just met you."

"Fair play."

Nothing was said for several minutes, then Archie

glanced over again and said, "You have a very interesting file."

"I have a file?"

"Only in my office."

"And what office is that?"

Archie chuckled. "Let's just say I help look after the security of our nation."

"Steve was right."

"He doesn't seem to like me."

"He's an ex-cop." John turned to look at Archie. "He's probably learnt from experience."

"Ha!" Instead of taking offense, Archie seemed highly amused. "We're not all bad guys, you know."

"Well, as I said, I judge a man by his deeds, and so far, all you've done is talk."

"Touché." Archie slowed and pulled over to the right to allow an *Eléctrico*, one of Lisbon's electric trams, space to rumble past.

Once past, Archie pulled out again and continued on his way. "Why don't I start with telling you what I know?" He glanced at John. "How about that?"

John shrugged.

"Yesterday morning Adriana D'Silva was seized by three Chinese men dressed in black and bundled into the back of a stolen van." He eyed John expectantly.

"I know. I was there."

"Yes. She was then taken to Popham Airfield and flown in a Cessna Stationair to an airfield north of here, where the flight was met by members of local law enforcement. Unfortunately, the passengers claimed diplomatic immunity, and they left in a vehicle registered to the Chinese Embassy here in Lisbon. However, there was no sign of Ms. D'Silva." Again, he looked at John for confirmation.

John nodded, but said nothing.

"But that was enough for you to jump on a flight and come here to find her."

John stared out the window, neither acknowledging nor denying.

"And we now have a witness who says she was held captive in a shipping container in the warehouse we just left."

"Yes."

"So she *was* on that flight."

"She was in a large bag."

"Hmmm." Archie drove in silence for a little longer and then said, "Coincidentally," he again looked over at John, "or not, a Chinese businessman by the name of Xie Longwei disappeared about seven months ago from the Atwell Estate a short distance from where Ms. D'Silva was snatched. And again coincidentally, Ms. D'Silva wrote a series of articles about Mr. Xie, the Golden Fortune Corporation, and the influence of the Chinese Communist Party in Africa. Am I right so far?"

"Carry on."

"So I believe there's a connection. I just don't know what it is."

John didn't reply.

"At first I thought it was revenge," Archie continued. "But I don't think so now. In fact, I reached out to certain individuals in the... Chinese Government, and they knew nothing about the kidnapping." He sighed. "There's also the matter of your involvement."

"Adriana is my girlfriend."

"Yes, I'm aware of that." Archie slowed and turned into Rua Jau, then turned right through the ornate iron gates of the Pestana Palace Hotel. "I'm referring to the incidents surrounding your parents, the arson attack on their cottage, and..." he pulled to a stop outside the hotel and turned to look at John. "The gunfight at the estate in the middle of the night."

John continued staring out the windshield. "And what makes you think that has anything to do with me?"

Archie chuckled. "Call it a hunch. Based on your past."

"My past?"

A doorman approached to open John's door and Archie dismissed him with a wave of his hand.

"You're either a very unlucky man, John, or..."

"Or what?"

Archie exhaled loudly. "I don't know, to be honest. I mean, there's Oman, Syria, Sri Lanka, India. Controversy follows you around, John." He shrugged. "And so do dead bodies."

John tried not to show any reaction. This guy seemed to know far too much about his life.

"John, I don't care about the dead bodies. They were all bad guys. Collateral damage, as my friends from across the pond like to call it. Look..." He turned in his seat and fixed his gaze on John. "I know what Xie was up to. Golden Fortune was a front for the CCP's Belt and Road program in Africa. So when he disappeared, I thought good riddance to bad rubbish. I thought the matter was over. But now Ms. D' Silva's kidnapping seems to indicate that it isn't. Would you care to comment?"

John leaned forward and looked into the side-view mirror. He saw Steve pull up behind them in the X5. He wished he could speak to him, seek his advice. How much could he share with this guy? Should he trust him at all?

He sat back in his seat and tapped a rhythm on his thigh with the fingers of his right hand.

"Why should I trust you?"

"Good question. A good question indeed."

John waited for an answer and when one wasn't immediately forthcoming, he turned to look at the man sitting beside him. Archie was watching an elderly couple make their way down the steps from the hotel lobby.

Once they had gone, he turned to face John. "Trust has to be earned, John. I know that. Believe it or not, my work with the... Ministry of Foreign Affairs..." he winked, "depends a lot on trust. I operate in the murky corners, but the people I work with know that when I give my word, they can depend on me. Without that, I wouldn't have lasted this long. So when I give my word that I'll help you, I mean it."

John nodded thoughtfully. "So my next question is why?"

Archie smiled. "Because I will not have the communists operating on my soil. When Xie was running his operations in Africa from Atwell Estate..." He shook his head. "What he did to that beautiful house is unforgivable... anyway... we turned a blind eye. But kidnapping Ms D'Silva on English soil is crossing a line that should never be crossed. My ancestors fought hard to make our country what it is and I will not stand for these CCP shenanigans. It's time I taught the *Guojia Anquan Bu* a lesson."

Steve appeared beside John's door, bent down, and looked inside. He glared at Archie, then gave John a questioning look. John held up a finger, telling him to wait, and then turned back to Archie. He wasn't getting anywhere by himself, so maybe it was time to take a leap of faith.

"Okay. I'll take a chance and trust you."

Archie nodded.

"Adriana is being held hostage until we release Xie."

To give Archie credit, he didn't seem surprised. "I see."

John waited for him to say something else. He didn't have to wait long.

"So... do you have Xie?"

"No."

"Oh." Archie pursed his lips. "Hmmm. So who does have Xie?"

"No-one. He's dead."

"That's rather inconvenient."

64

The shadows were growing long again when Adriana heard footsteps on the stairs and the bolt on the door sliding back. For the past hour, she had alternated between dozing on the bed and pacing around the room, trying to speed up the passing of time. Her stomach rumbled with hunger and she had a pressing need to empty her bladder.

The door swung open, and the strange Chinese woman stood in the doorway. She held a small pistol in one hand and a bottle of water in the other.

"I need to use the bathroom."

The woman stared at her, then nodded. She made a beckoning motion with the pistol. "This way."

Adriana stood and walked toward the woman.

"If you try anything, I'll shoot you."

"I know," Adriana replied.

The woman tossed the bottle of water onto the bedroom floor, then backed out of the doorway and waited in the hallway.

She was much smaller than Adriana and for a moment

she contemplated rushing her and overpowering her. But the barrel of the pistol never wavered, and she knew she wouldn't make it two steps before her stomach filled with bullets. She paused in the doorway. "Where is it?"

The woman jerked her head to her left and took another step backwards. Adriana nodded, turned right, walked several paces down the hallway and stopped outside a door. "This one?"

"The one behind you."

Adriana turned around and pushed open the door. Inside was a w/c with an overhead cistern and beside it was a cracked and grimy bathtub. There was a window set high in the wall, but it was too high and too small for her to climb out of. She stepped inside, then turned to close the door.

"Leave the door open."

"I need some privacy."

There was no reply, so Adriana shrugged, unzipped her pants and settled onto the seat.

As she closed her eyes, a wave of relief washed over her as her bladder emptied. A cough broke the silence, and she opened her eyes, half-expecting to see the woman standing in the doorway, but she was nowhere to be seen. Instead, the creak of the floorboards suggested she was near the door frame but just out of sight.

"Why?"

There was no reply.

Adriana tried again. "Is it something I wrote?"

The woman scoffed. "You really think you're so important?"

"Then explain to me why? Why am I here?"

There was another creak of floorboards, and the woman appeared in the doorway. Her lip twisted into a sneer as she aimed the pistol squarely at Adriana's face.

"Because your boyfriend took something from me," she declared.

Adriana stared down the barrel of the weapon.

"My boyfriend? John?"

"Yes. John," she spat the name. "John Hayes. And now I've got something of his."

Adriana wanted to keep her talking, anything to take her mind off the weapon.

"What did he take?"

"You really don't know?" The woman shook her head in disbelief. "He took the only man I've ever loved."

Adriana's brow furrowed in confusion. Then, slowly, comprehension dawned. "Are you...? Do you mean...?"

"Yes. Xie Longwei. A greater man than your lover will ever be. But he's coming back to me. All I needed was some leverage. Something John Hayes is prepared to risk everything for."

Adriana swallowed hard. As far as she knew, Xie was dead, but John must have worked something out.

"So it's good news, right?" Adriana asked hopefully. "You'll get what you want and then you'll let me go."

The woman cackled with laughter. Her eyes were wide, and slightly bloodshot.

"That's what he thinks, my dear. That's what he thinks."

That didn't sound too good. Adriana needed time to think. "Can I stand up? I've finished."

The woman's manic expression eased, and she nodded, taking two paces back.

Adriana stood, fastened her pants, then nodded toward the washbasin. "I'm going to wash my hands."

The woman grunted, and Adriana walked over to the basin, turning on the tap. She studied her reflection in the mirror as the tap sputtered brown water. The mention of

John had filled her with hope, but the stress of the last two days showed in the dark circles under her eyes and deep lines of strain creasing her forehead. She leaned down, checked the water was running clear, and splashed her face.

But what did she mean by 'that's what he thinks'?

Troubled by the remark, Adriana straightened up, wiping away the excess water with her hands before running them through her hair.

"You still look beautiful. Now turn around."

Adriana turned to face the woman, who now held a cell phone in her spare hand.

"Smile."

Adriana frowned. Smiling was the last thing on her mind.

"He wants proof of life," the woman explained, then chuckled. "Let's keep him happy for a little while longer."

65

It had been Archie's suggestion to request for proof-of-life. The four men sat inside his suite, surrounded by the remnants of a very late room-service lunch scattered across the dining table. As Archie spoke on the house phone, organizing a round of coffee and for someone to clear the plates, John's phone buzzed. Retrieving it from his pocket, he tapped the screen.

There she was, his Adriana, staring back at him. Confused, irritated... and tired.

A wave of emotions washed over him: relief, frustration, and finally, anger. Quickly, he forwarded the photograph to Ramesh with instructions to gather whatever information he could, then addressed the room.

"They've sent a photo."

Steve and Archie gathered around and looked over his shoulder at the screen.

"She looks okay," Steve reassured John. "Tired but okay."

John frowned and nodded at the same time.

"Does the background look familiar?" Archie asked.

"No," John shook his head.

"Zoom in."

Using his fingers, John enlarged the photo on the screen, and the three men studied the photograph.

"She's in a bathroom," Steve muttered. "Tiled walls and..." he pointed at the screen, "that mirror."

The edge of a mirror was visible over her shoulder and John zoomed in closer, moving the photo around with his finger until the mirror took up most of the screen.

"It's her."

Reflected in the mirror was a Chinese woman, a gun in one hand, and the phone in the other. The image wasn't clear, but John knew who it was.

"Who?"

"Wang Mingmei."

Archie reached out for the phone and John handed it over.

While he studied the screen, John explained, "She was Xie's assistant. I met her once. On the estate. I tried to meet Xie and was intercepted by his security. They took me to meet her. She questioned me for a bit, then kicked me off the property. I never got to see him."

He noticed Archie doing something with the phone.

"What are you doing?"

Archie looked up. "I'm sending it to my number. I'll get someone to trace it."

John nodded. He decided not to mention Ramesh.

"My gut feeling is this is her operation, not the government's." Archie looked from Steve to John. "My Chinese contact knew nothing about the kidnapping."

"Do you trust him?"

"Ha. Not at all," Archie scoffed. "But body language doesn't lie. He genuinely knew nothing about it."

John was nodding slowly. "So that explains the fake

embassy plates on the vehicle at the airport."

"So, who were the kidnappers, then?"

John shrugged. "Probably Triads. They'll do anything for money."

"Yes," Archie agreed. "The CCP uses them all the time. Whenever they want deniability."

The phone buzzed again, and Archie handed it back. "You're getting another message."

John tapped on the screen. Any joy at seeing Adriana swiftly evaporated. "She wants a photo of Xie."

"Shit," Steve cursed.

John stared at the message, wondering how the hell he was going to deal with this. He started typing.

"What are you saying?" Archie asked.

"I'm stalling her. Telling her he's not with us right now."

"That will only work for a little while," said Steve.

"I know." John sighed. "That's why we have to come up with a solution quickly."

As if hearing John's comment, the phone buzzed again.

You've got three hours or I'll cut off a finger.

"Fuck." John cursed, then held up the screen so all could see.

"Fuck," Steve repeated, followed by an 'oh dear' from Archie.

John felt numb, his gaze fixed on a spot on the wall. It was all his fault. Once again, someone he cared about was suffering because of something he had done.

A hand landed on his shoulder, and he heard Steve's voice as if from a distance. "We'll figure something out, mate. We always do."

Though he heard the words, they didn't quite register. His phone buzzed in his hand, and in a daze, he brought it to his ear. "Hello."

The Chinese Cat

There was no response.

"It's a message, John," said Steve.

John frowned and shook the fog from his head. He glanced at the phone screen. Steve was right. A message from Ramesh.

Call me.

John dialed Ramesh's number, then stepped away to the far side of the room, holding the phone to his ear.

"What is it?" he asked in a hushed tone. "Please, tell me you've got some good news."

"I've found her," Ramesh responded, barely able to contain his excitement.

"What? How?" John exclaimed, drawing the attention of everyone in the room.

"I checked the EXIF data in the photo. Like most people, she hasn't changed her security settings, so I know the time of the photo, what type of phone, and more importantly, the location."

"Where?"

"I'll send you the co-ordinates. She's about a hundred and fifty kilometers north of you, near the coast."

"Excellent. See if you can get me any maps, photos, satellite images. Anything that can help."

"I'm on it."

"Good work, my friend." John ended the call and turned to face the room.

Archie was watching him curiously. "Who was that?"

John saw Steve was about to say something.

"A friend," John said before Steve mentioned Ramesh. John was only trusting Archie up to a point. There was no need for him to know everything.

"What's important is we know where she is."

66

"Send Wei in!" Anson Liu growled, then slammed the phone back onto the desk. The wretched woman had gone dark, seemingly vanishing off the face of the earth. How the hell did a middle-aged secretary evade the best of Chinese surveillance?

If his team didn't find her soon, he too would be sent back to China to spend the rest of his life shuffling papers in some god-forsaken country town in the middle of no-where. He shuddered at the thought.

There was a tap on the door, and Anson looked up as Wei poked his head through the gap in the door.

"Well?"

Wei stepped inside and closed the door behind him. "The other man is a Danny Chan. Portuguese citizen. But he's a nobody. Unemployed until Wang gave him this job. He's not been home since this morning."

"Dead?"

Wei shrugged. "We don't know for sure, but I don't think so. He called his mother, saying he wouldn't be home for a while. So my guess is he's hiding."

"Phone?"

"The last known location was a fuel station on the outskirts of Lisbon, but the phone's gone dead."

Anson ground his teeth together, struggling to keep control of his temper.

"And the other men? The kidnapping team?"

"*Sun Yee On.* A team out of France. They're saying they were told it was a government sanctioned operation."

"They would," Anson sneered. "Their only loyalty is to the one who pays the most."

Wei remained silent.

"So what you're saying is we have nothing?"

The only movement in Wei's face was a slight twitch under his left eye.

"*Cào nǐ mā!*" Anson roared, slamming his fist down on the desk.

This time Wei flinched.

"If you don't find her soon, I'm taking you back to China with me." He raised his fist and jabbed a finger at Wei. "So make sure you've got everyone working on this. There's no way this *sān bā* is going to get away."

Anson's cell phone buzzed and shifted across the desk. He picked it up, still glaring at Wei, then glanced at the screen.

Wei was moving toward the door, and Anson called out, "Wait."

A friend of yours?

Below the message was a photo of a beautiful but hassled looking Western woman. Partly visible on the wall behind her was a mirror with a figure reflected in the glass. The reflected figure had been marked with a circle and a question mark.

Anson enlarged the photo, beckoned Wei closer, then

held up the phone so he could see the screen. "The *lao wai men*, the foreigners, have found her!"

67

Archie arranged for a laptop to be brought up from the hotel business center, and the three men gathered around it, examining satellite images of the coordinates provided by Ramesh.

The farmhouse stood isolated amid fields in the countryside northwest of Lisbon, in a region known as the Beira Litoral. A dirt farm track stretched about a kilometer from the main road to reach the house, with the nearest neighbor located several fields away.

"How do we approach it without being seen? The land is flat all around. She'll see us coming from a mile away."

John stared at the screen. Steve was right.

"Perhaps we could approach at night?" Steve continued hopefully.

John grimaced. "The problem is we know nothing about the place. Does she have security? If so, are they armed? Do they have night vision capability?" He shook his head. "Much as I want to go in as soon as possible..." he looked at each of the men in turn, "I don't want anyone to get hurt."

Archie was silent. He stood staring at the laptop, his

arms folded across his chest, the forefinger of his right hand tapping a slow rhythm on his chin.

"What do you think, Archie?" John asked. "You said you would help us. What can you bring to the table?"

"I'm thinking," was all he said.

"Can't you call in a strike team? The SAS? Raid the house in the small hours?"

Archie took a deep breath, his shoulders rising as he inhaled. "If only it was so easy," he mumbled, still staring at the screen. "We're not in England anymore. There are protocols... I would need to get it cleared..." he trailed off as if he had been talking to himself the whole time.

Steve caught John's eye. He rolled his eyes and shook his head.

John agreed. It was down to them, just as it had been from the beginning.

"Can you at least get me some equipment?"

"Equipment?"

"Night-vision equipment? Some weapons?"

Archie turned to look at John, a grin slowly spreading across his face. "So, I was right about you all along." He winked. "Let me make a few calls."

John watched him walk away to the far side of the room, then looked at Steve.

"Are you in?"

"I told you, mate. I'm not leaving until we get her back."

"Good." John smiled. "Thank you."

John's phone vibrated again, this time with an incoming call. He checked the screen, then turned it so that Steve could see the name.

Both Steve's eyebrows shot up in surprise.

"Keep Archie up that end," John told him, then held the phone to his ear.

"Hello."

"John, it's Joseph."

"Hi."

"Are you... with someone?"

John moved to the back of the room, his eyes on Archie. "I'm not alone. I can listen, but may be limited in what I can say."

"Understood. I will arrive at your location in just over six hours with our friend."

"Our friend?" John couldn't hide his surprise. Lost for words for a moment, he turned away so no-one in the room could see his expression. "I... I thought he was dead."

"Yes, well, I never said he was dead. I said he didn't exist, which, according to the rest of the world, is technically correct. I'm sorry John. My hands were tied. I had to seek special permission."

"I understand. Thank you."

"But there is one condition, John."

"Okay."

"No-one can ever know of our involvement."

"Understood. You have my word."

"Good. I'll text you when I arrive."

"Thank you again, my friend."

"I think maybe we're even after this," Joseph chuckled.

"I agree. Oh, do me a favor. I need proof of life. Otherwise, they'll start cutting off her fingers."

"Oh no... a photo?"

"Yeah."

"He... ah... doesn't look his best."

"As long as he's breathing."

"Sending it now."

John ended the call and turned around. Archie was still on the phone at the far end of the room. Danny was lying on the bed staring at the muted TV screen and Steve was hovering mid-way, trying unsuccessfully to look like he was doing something useful.

John caught his eye, and with a jerk of his head, summoned him over. The two men met beside the table and leaned over the laptop as if discussing something on the screen.

"New development." John muttered. The phone buzzed in his hand, and he turned the screen so Steve could see it.

"Who's that?"

"Xie Longwei."

68

"Good news chaps."

Archie strolled across the room to where John and Steve were studying the satellite images on the laptop.

"I've rustled up a set of NVGs and two Glock 17s with an extra magazine each."

"That's it?" Steve asked in disbelief. "Are you sure you work for MI6?"

"I don't think I ever said that, my antipodean friend." Archie grinned at Steve. "But what I will say is these weapons are clean and untraceable."

"They'll do," John grunted. "When can we get them?"

"They'll be delivered here to the hotel in under an hour."

"Good. Thank you." John glanced at Steve before continuing. "While you were on the phone, there's been a development."

"Oh, really? What do you mean?"

John held up his phone so Archie could see the photo of Xie.

"Is that..." Archie peered at the screen. "Is he alive? Hard to tell from that photo."

"He's alive, and I'll exchange him for Adriana tomorrow."

"But..." Archie tilted his head to one side and frowned. " I thought he was dead. Where's he been all this time?"

"It doesn't matter. What matters is he's here now. I'll swap him for Adriana and hopefully this will all be over."

"Hopefully?"

John shrugged. "Until Adriana is safe and well, I won't let my guard down." He eyeballed Archie. "Which is why I'll take those weapons."

"I see. What time and where?"

"I'm just about to set that up."

John typed a message to Mingmei, attached Xie's photo and clicked send. Looking up, he explained, "I learnt from her mistake today. So I got a friend to scrub the EXIF data from the image before sending it."

"Good."

"I've also told her we'll make the exchange tomorrow morning."

"Why so soon?"

John looked at him as if he was mad. "Because the sooner I get Adriana back, the better."

"Yes, of course, I just thought you wanted more time to reconnoitre the farm?"

John shook his head. "Steve and I have seen enough. There's nothing to be gained by delaying. As soon as those weapons are here, Archie, we'll be off."

"And what's my role in this grand caper?"

John nodded toward Danny, who was now curled up asleep on the bed. "Watch him and make sure he doesn't run away before we've made the handover. I don't want him warning anyone, even if it's by mistake."

"Oh. I see." All the humor drained from his face, only to be replaced by a look of disappointment.

But that wasn't John's problem. His sole aim was to get Adriana back, not to keep people happy.

69

Mingmei's cheeks glistened with tears as she whispered, "What have they done to you?" She gazed at the photo on her phone, then gently brushed her fingertips over Xie's face. "Soon you will be safe, my dear."

Closing her eyes, she felt a warmth fill her body. After months of searching, her beloved would finally be back with her. Despite the stress, fear, and sadness of the past few months, it was all worth it. Tomorrow morning, if all went well, they would be together. She still couldn't believe it was actually happening, and she vowed to never let him out of her sight again.

Her eyes snapped open, and she looked up at the wall in front of her. It was covered in papers, documents, and maps, many of them with torn corners from her hasty escape from the last hideout.

She visualized how it would unfold, scanning the wall for anything that might go wrong. Despite her lack of trust in John Hayes, she was convinced she held the upper hand. He would never risk the life of the woman he loved. Of that, she was sure.

She stood and walked over to the desk at the foot of the wall, sliding open a drawer to retrieve a plastic folder. Opening it up, she checked the contents: two US passports, driving licenses from the state of California, birth certificates, social security numbers, and credit cards, all issued in the name of Mr. and Mrs. Hui.

She had paid handsomely for these new identities, but money would never be an issue for the couple. She still had access to numbered accounts in tax havens around the world, providing more than enough resources for them to live comfortably for the rest of their lives.

As she examined the documents, she heard someone clearing their throat. Quickly closing the file, she turned around to face them.

"You called for me?"

Mingmei studied the man in the doorway. He was big, over six feet, and almost too wide to fit through the doorway. A thick beard covered the lower part of his face and a pair of wraparound sunglasses were perched on the brim of a faded baseball cap.

"Ricky, I'm expecting our visitors around six a.m tomorrow."

"Earlier than expected, Ma'am?"

"Yes, but everything else will be the same."

"Understood. We're ready. We know exactly what to do."

"Good. I want everyone to be on high alert. Do you need more men?"

"No, we're good." Ricky frowned. "Are you expecting trouble?"

"No."

The truth was, she wasn't sure. She had underestimated John Hayes before and didn't want to make the same mistake again. But Ricky seemed to know what he was doing. "Your final payment will be wired to your account as soon as the visitors leave."

"Understood."

Mingmei continued staring at him until he got the message.

"Okay, I'll go then." He backed out of the door, the AR15 dangling on its one-point sling, knocking against the door frame as he turned around.

Mingmei had opted not to use Chinese security for this last part of her operation because of the high risk of leaks. Instead, she had enlisted a team of Romanian mercenaries led by Ricărdel Popescu. The team comprised six members in total, with Ricky, as he preferred to be known, organizing them into four-hour shifts: four men on patrol and two resting. He claimed to be ex-*Brigada Specială de Operații,* Romanian Special Forces, but Mingmei wasn't concerned about his background. All she cared about was their ability to handle firearms and to not ask questions.

70

John slowed the X5 and turned off the N247-5 and into the Cascais Municipal Aerodrome. He followed the road for a short way and entered the carpark, which sat deserted at two in the morning except for a black van stationed near the fence. Across from it stood a sleek white Gulfstream G550, unmarked save for its tail number.

As John drove in, the van by the fence flashed its lights twice.

John drove over, pulled up in front of the van, then backed the X5 into the space beside it.

Keeping the engine running, he rolled down his window and glanced over. The passenger window lowered, revealing a grinning Joseph Tamba.

Joseph had changed little since their last encounter, still resembling a Ralph Lauren model, albeit with hints of gray creeping into his neatly trimmed hair.

"Great to see you, John," Joseph greeted him warmly.

"I just wish it were under better circumstances, Joseph,"

John replied, noticing Joseph's smile falter as he glanced over John's shoulder.

"This is Steve. I trust him with my life."

"That's good enough for me, John," Joseph chuckled, the sound coming as a low rumble. "Nice to meet you, Steve."

Steve raised a hand in greeting. "I've heard a lot about you, mate. The pleasure is all mine."

Joseph leaned back in his seat so John could see his driver.

"I'm sure you remember Moses?"

"How can I forget?" John opened the door and climbed out. Joseph did the same and John reached out to shake his hand, only to be pulled into an embrace with a few hard slaps on the back that almost took John's breath away and reawakened the bruising across his shoulders.

John extricated himself, took a step back, and asked, "Where's our friend?"

Joseph slid the side door of the van open. Just visible in the ambient light from the street lamps was a hooded and bound figure in an orange prison jumpsuit.

"I thought he should be suitably dressed for the exchange."

"Hmmm," John murmured, taking a step forward and lifting the hood to reveal the man's face. He was a mere shadow of the man who had caused so much grief for his parents. His frame had shrunk, appearing to be only half his former weight, and he seemed to have aged twenty years. Sparse stubble dotted his sunken cheeks, and his skin was pallid and gray, as if he hadn't seen sunlight in ages.

"He won't trouble you. We sedated him for the flight and just gave him another dose before you arrived."

"How long will he be out for?" John asked. "I need him walking by six a.m."

"It'll wear off in a couple of hours. He'll be groggy but will walk."

"Good. Let's get him in the car." John opened the back door of the X5 and then watched as Joseph picked up Xie and tossed him onto the back seat of the X5 as if he weighed nothing.

John closed the door and extended his hand. "Thank you, Joseph. I know how difficult this must have been for you. But Adriana means everything to me."

Joseph clasped his hand in both of his. "I hope I get to meet her one day, John. May God protect you."

"Thank you, Joseph." John waved at Moses, then climbed back into the BMW.

Joseph walked up to the door and leaned a powerful forearm on the windowsill. "Remember what I said, John. No-one must ever know."

"I give you my word, Joseph."

Joseph nodded and smiled. He slapped John on the shoulder, nodded at Steve, then stepped back as John put the car in gear and pulled out of the parking space.

71

John drove steadily for two hours north along the A8, carefully staying just below the speed limit. He was keen to avoid any encounters with the police, especially with a body in the back seat.

Throughout the journey, the two men spoke little, each lost in his own thoughts. Despite having rehearsed their plan extensively, they were aware that a considerable portion of their success would rely on luck.

Just after four a.m., John turned off the A8 and onto the narrower N109, heading westward through the towns of Coimbrao and Barreiro. The roads lay deserted, and even in the towns, there was little activity aside from the occasional stray dog and several cats.

Just before the coast, John turned north again, taking a minor road lined with pines and cypress. The road narrowed further, becoming a single lane, and the trees gave way to shrubs and patches of open ground. After several kilometers, John took another turn, this time heading inland and slowed while Steve double checked the GPS.

"About a hundred metres further ahead," he said and peered through the windshield.

John dimmed the lights and crawled slowly along the road until Steve told him to stop. John pulled over, turned off the engine, and checked his watch. It was four thirty. On schedule. He shifted in his seat to get a better look at Steve.

"It's not too late to back out, Steve. I won't think any less of you if you do."

"I'm not backing out, mate. I'll be here to the end."

John nodded, then reached over and gripped Steve's shoulder. "Thanks, mate. Be careful."

Steve grinned as he reached behind the seat for the sports bag he had stowed earlier.

"I'm always careful," he replied as he placed the bag on his lap and unzipped it. Inside were the night vision goggles Archie had supplied and both the Glocks. Steve removed a Glock and slipped it into his jacket pocket, then stuffed a spare magazine in the other. He then opened a tin of black boot polish and began applying it to his face, neck, and the back of his hands.

Both men were dressed identically in black jeans, black Salomon boots and lightweight black bomber jackets. With Steve's skin blackened, there was no way anyone would see him in the darkness.

"What do you think?" Steve asked when he'd finished.

"A definite improvement."

"I'm looking like Ramesh now."

"I'll tell him you said that."

"Thanks, mate." Steve hesitated, suddenly serious. "Well, I'd better get going then. See you in a couple of hours."

"Call me when you're in position."

Steve nodded, pulled the NVGs over his head, and

climbed out of the car. He closed the door gently until it clicked, adjusted the NVGs and then disappeared into the undergrowth.

72

An hour passed, and John grew restless. He stood outside the vehicle, leaning against the front fender, immersed in the sounds of the night. The air was cool and crisp and tasted of salt. Crickets chirped, leaves rustled in the wind, and an early bird broke the silence with its call. The absence of light pollution revealed a sky filled with a billion stars. John scanned the heavens, identifying the familiar constellation of Ursa Major and spotting the bright glow of Venus in the east. John felt a movement of the car and he glanced back at Xie still unconscious on the rear seat. The sedative must be wearing off, as he had changed position twice in the last ten minutes.

The phone buzzed in John's pocket and he took it out and held it to his ear.

"I can see the house," Steve whispered. "I'm about a hundred metres from the front."

"Any problems getting there?"

"Nah mate, these NVGs are brilliant. Feels like daylight... except everything is green. Wait one sec..."

The line went quiet and all John could hear was Steve's breathing.

"Yeah, mate, there are guards. I've counted three. I reckon there's probably one more. Looks like one on each side of the house."

"Armed?"

"Yeah. Automatic weapons, not pistols."

"Shit." John exhaled loudly. "Well, nothing we didn't expect."

"Nope. Look, I'm going to get closer. The Glock won't be much good at this range."

"Be careful, Steve. I need you as a lookout."

"I know. Don't worry. I'm a big boy. I know what to do. Call you back in a bit."

The line went dead and John climbed back into the car. There was an uneasy feeling in his stomach, and his heart was beating faster than it should. He took a deep breath, forcing himself to stay calm. In another thirty minutes, he would drive onto the farm.

Xie stirred and mumbled on the back seat, and John turned, reached back and slapped him. "Hey, wake up."

Xie muttered something again and changed position.

John stepped out of the car once more, opened the back door, and leaned in to grasp Xie by the shoulders. He pulled him into a sitting position, removing the hood from his head. Xie blinked twice and looked around, a vacant expression on his face.

John slapped his cheeks once, twice, a third time. That seemed to work, as some clarity appeared in his eyes. He frowned, then peered at John. He stared at him for a long time, then spoke, his voice hoarse as if he hadn't used it in a very long time.

"I know you."

"Do you?" John asked.

"I think so. You look familiar." Xie tried to move his arms, then realized they were bound behind his back. He looked down at the orange jumpsuit, then, still puzzled, looked up at John. "Why am I here?"

John didn't know what to say. This wasn't the Xie he remembered, the one he had grown to despise. This was a bewildered old man, a far cry from the arrogant businessman who had ruled Golden Fortune with an iron fist. John almost felt sorry for him.

Almost.

This man was responsible for the kidnapping of the woman he loved and there was no room for sympathy.

John closed the door on him and climbed back into the front of the vehicle, pushing all thoughts of sympathy to the back of his mind.

73

The minute hand crept towards the top of the hour, each passing minute feeling like an eternity.

Above, the stars gradually faded as the sky transitioned from black to gray. Sunrise was still half an hour away, but the first hints of daylight were starting to emerge.

Despite being awake all night, John was wired as adrenaline coursed through his system.

He had chosen the time for two reasons. He wanted darkness to allow Steve to approach unnoticed, but he also needed enough light for the handover. Early morning was the best compromise.

He tapped his earbuds and spoke, "All good, Steve?"

"Yeah. I'm in position. There's a stone wall on the left near the front of the house. I'm behind that."

"Okay. Any activity?"

"Yeah, they're getting ready. Lights on in the house and the guards are more active."

"Right. I'm coming in now."

"Good luck, mate. I'm watching for you."

"Stay on line."

John glanced in the rearview mirror at his passenger. Xie dozed on the back seat, his head slumped on his chest. He'd barely moved since John had woken him half an hour earlier. The sedative Joseph had used must have been very strong.

John took a deep breath, started the engine, and pulled out onto the road. He drove on for around a kilometer, then spotted the dirt track that led up to the farmhouse. Pulling to a stop, he double-checked the location against the GPS—it wouldn't do to turn up at the wrong farmhouse. Satisfied he was in the correct place, he leaned over and removed the remaining Glock from the open sports bag on the passenger seat. He wedged it under his right thigh and slipped the spare magazine into his jacket pocket and zipped it up.

With one last glance in the mirror at his passenger, he turned up the track.

The surface was rough and uneven, and John was relieved he had rented the SUV. It navigated most of the track effortlessly, although he still had to focus to avoid the deepest ruts. One particularly rough patch caused Xie to tumble onto his side, waking him and prompting him to grumble in Mandarin. John checked on him through the rearview mirror, but left him lying there.

The sky was visibly lighter and now John could see the fields on either side without the use of the headlights. Crumbling dry stone walls lined both sides of the track, punctuated occasionally by rotten wooden gates. Everything was falling apart as if the property had been abandoned years ago.

A voice in his ear announced, "I can see your lights."

"I can see the farmhouse now," John replied as the lights of the building appeared at the end of the track.

Powerful headlights flashed on, blinding him, and he cursed, pulling to a stop. He waited for a moment and then the headlights dimmed, leaving spots in his vision. He waited until they cleared, then edged the BMW slowly forward.

"What can you see, Steve?"

"They've got the van facing you. Those were the lights. All four guards are in front now. Two on each side. All armed."

"Mingmei?"

"I've seen her once. She's back in the house now."

"Okay, here we go."

John stopped the X5 and positioned it at an angle to block the track, but also so the bulk of the vehicle provided him with cover when he got out.

The track continued for another thirty metres before it opened up into a patch of gravel in front of the house. There was a black van facing him and a blue Volkswagen parked to the right. John stayed in the car and studied the house. It was two levels, built of brick and stone under a tiled roof. Even in the low light of dawn it was clear the house had seen better days. He could see the guards now, too. Four men in black, weapons raised.

John was aware of his heart rate spiking and he took several deep breaths, trying to calm himself.

"You'll be okay, mate," said the reassuring voice in his ear.

John looked to his left but couldn't see Steve anywhere. That was good.

"I'm getting out."

"Copy."

Keeping the engine running, John opened the door and with the Glock in his hand, slid out, keeping the car between him and the guards. He spotted movement through the window and saw a diminutive figure appear in the front doorway of the farmhouse.

Mingmei.

"The woman is out," Steve confirmed.

"I see her." John moved toward the rear passenger door, opened it, and grabbed hold of Xie's feet. Xie had lost so much weight, John easily dragged him across the seat with one hand.

He ignored Xie's feeble protests, and once his legs were out of the vehicle, John grabbed him by the shoulder of his jumpsuit and pulled him upright.

He slapped him twice, once on each side of the face, his skin flushing red against his sickly gray pallor. "Come on. I need you awake."

Xie's old spirit surfaced as he glared at John and uttered something in Mandarin that probably wasn't polite.

John didn't speak Mandarin, but knew a few Cantonese curse words from his time in Hong Kong. *"Fai di la, diu lei lo mo!"*

Xie's eyes widened.

John spun him around, grabbing a handful of the back of his jumpsuit with his left hand and jabbing him in the side of his head with the barrel of the Glock. He pushed him toward the front of the vehicle, keeping him close, using his body as a shield. Just ahead of the driver's door, he stopped. The guards could see Xie but if they started firing, John could drop below the hood and use the engine block as shelter.

The headlights of the van flicked back on full beam, blinding him again.

"Turn the fucking lights off," John shouted, turning his head away so as not to compromise his vision further.

The lights stayed on for several seconds, then turned off again.

"Bring him here," a male voice called out. He had an accent John couldn't place.

"Show me Adriana first," John countered, keeping the Glock pressed against Xie's head.

He peered around Xie and could see one of the men in conversation with Mingmei. The man then moved away, disappearing inside the house.

A moment later, he reappeared, pushing Adriana ahead of him. Despite the push, she maintained her composure, holding her head high. When he nudged her once more, she turned and said something. Judging by her expression, it wasn't polite.

John's heart skipped a beat, and he felt a warm feeling of relief wash over him.

"I'm here, baby!" he called out.

"John?" Adriana raised her head even higher. "I knew you would come."

"Let him go," the guard called out.

"You first," John countered. He watched the guard consult with Mingmei, then step forward.

"This is how we'll do it," he announced. "You bring him forward, I'll bring her forward. We'll do the exchange in the middle."

"Okay," John shouted. "But you start."

He heard the guard curse and saw him shake his head. He then reached out, grabbed Adriana by the arm, and pushed her in front of him. Adriana stumbled forward as he drew his handgun and pointed it at her back.

"*Filho da puta!*" she spat, and John grinned. Tightening his grip on the jumpsuit, he pulled Xie sideways, moving slowly around the hood of the car.

"Keep an eye on them, Steve," he muttered.

"Copy," came Steve's whispered reply in his ear.

John edged forward, matching his pace to that of Adriana and the guard, keeping Xie's body close to his, and the Glock pressed against his temple.

He peered out from the side so Adriana could see his face. "It's okay, Adriana. Everything is going to be okay."

"I know, John," she called back. "I trust you."

The guard growled something, and she cursed him again. He responded by pushing her forward again with his free hand, his pistol still trained on her midsection.

They were close now.

Xie had regained his senses and was no longer stumbling and tripping. He moved his head from side to side, taking in his surroundings.

"*Ni hai hao ma?* Are you okay?"

It was Mingmei's voice and his head whipped up, searching for her.

"*Nà shì shéi?*" he croaked. "Who's that?"

"Mingmei."

"Mingmei?" he stopped walking. "Mingmei?" he repeated.

"Yes, your girlfriend," John growled and pushed him forward. "Hurry up."

The guard pulled Adriana to a stop about ten paces from John, so John stopped, too.

"Let him go," the guard commanded.

John studied him. He was a big man, with a thick beard, possibly Eastern European, he wasn't sure. He kept his weapon trained on Adriana but wasn't concerned about using her as a shield.

"You first."

"I'm in charge here."

John shook his head. "You think you're in charge."

"I've got four guns to your one. I think we both know who's in charge."

"Do you really think I've come here alone? Are you such an idiot?"

Adriana smiled, her eyes fixed on John.

"Why do you think I wanted the exchange at this time? So my team could approach under the cover of darkness. Look around you. You're surrounded."

"Good one," Steve murmured in his ear.

"You're bluffing."

"Am I? Are you sure?"

The Beard glared back, but John could see his men looking around nervously and shifting position.

"You had better listen to him," Adriana added. "He doesn't bluff."

John pressed his advantage. "I have no interest in you or your men. I just want Adriana. Let her go and I'll let Xie go at the same time. Then I'll back away and return to my vehicle. Understood?"

The Beard glowered at him, but then nodded. "Go on then," he said and released his hold on Adriana.

She hesitated, searching for John's instruction. John encouraged her with a nod, and she stepped forward. John shoved Xie in front of him, at the same time stepping sideways, removing Adriana from his line of fire. He staggered his feet, turning his body slightly in a Weaver stance, his Glock pointed at the guard's head.

"Go to the car, Adriana," he called out, not taking his eyes off the bearded guard.

Once Adriana had moved past him, he began retreating, as the Beard did the same, pulling Xie back with him.

"She's safe," Steve confirmed, and John moved faster, his

The Chinese Cat

feet crunching in the gravel underfoot. He sensed the car behind him and glanced over his shoulder, making sure he knew where he was in relation to the car.

"Get in and lie down between the seats," he called out as he watched Mingmei hurry forward and wrap her arms around Xie.

John bumped up against the hood, and he allowed himself to relax slightly. Keeping his Glock pointed in the general direction of the house, he slid around the car toward the door.

He looked back at the house and frowned. All faces were turned in his direction.

"What's going on, Steve?"

No reply.

"Steve?"

Something cold and hard pressed against the back of John's head.

"Drop it."

74

Mingmei held Xie's arms and gazed up into his eyes. He was finally here with her. A tear escaped her eye, and embarrassed, she pulled him closer, wrapping her arms around him and burying her face in his chest as tears began to flow. Her nostrils filled with the sour smell of sweat and unfamiliar scents from another land, but she ignored it, happy it was finally over.

Releasing him, she stepped back, holding him at arm's length, and smiled at him. But there was no reciprocation. He stared at her blankly, as if she meant nothing to him. What had they done to him? She knew he would look different. She'd seen the photo. He was thinner and looked much older. But it wasn't just that. The man she once knew... he wasn't in there anymore.

"Longbaobao," she murmured. "Baby Dragon. It's me, Mingmei, your *baobei*. Your baby."

Xie blinked with confusion and looked around at the guards as if they could give him some clarity.

A rage ignited within Mingmei. She pushed him away and stepped back as the guard brought John and Adriana toward her. Her lip curled with disgust. What had the bastard *lao wai* done to her beloved?

"We found one in the fields," Ricky announced, gesturing toward another guard leading a captive toward them. The captive had his hands on his head, and from a distance, she initially mistook him for a black man. However, as they approached, she realized he had black paint on his face.

The black painted man spoke—an Australian, "Sorry mate. I missed these two."

"It's okay," John Hayes replied, but his eyes were locked with hers.

She ignored the Australian and stepped closer to the Devil.

"John Hayes," she spat the name as if the words tasted bad in her mouth. "So you thought you could get the better of me?" A wicked smirk danced on her lips. "You forgot one thing. Not only are we superior to you *lao wai men*, we are patient. We are prepared to wait a lifetime for our revenge." She stopped speaking and a series of erratic giggles escaped her lips. "But it didn't take me that long."

John Hayes didn't react. His face was expressionless, and the sight fueled the rage bubbling away inside her. She looked over his shoulder at Adriana, and her eyes gleamed. Reaching into the handbag slung over her shoulder, she pulled out her SIG. Walking over to Xie, she thrust it into his hand, then pulled him in front of John and Adriana.

"Now it's time for you to experience what I went through," she cackled.

She tugged on Xie's jumpsuit sleeve. "Do it."

Xie stared at the weapon in his hand as if not registering what it was, then looked up at Mingmei with a puzzled look on his face.

Mingmei snarled, grabbed his arm and lifted it in the air, extending it so that Xie was pointing the SIG Sauer at Adriana. "Kill the bitch!" she screamed.

John stepped in front of Adriana as Steve lunged forward, only to be felled to the ground by a rifle butt to the back of his head.

"Kill her!" she screamed again, this time stamping her foot on the ground.

A guard pulled John to one side, affording Xie a clear line of sight, but he wasn't looking at Adriana. He was staring at Mingmei in complete confusion.

She stepped in front of him, grabbed a handful of his jumpsuit, and pulled him close to her until his face was inches from hers. "Kill. That. Bitch!"

He blinked as saliva spattered his face, and then his expression changed. He looked up, found Adriana, and straightened his arm.

There was a sound like an angry bee, then his head exploded, flesh and brain matter splattering all over Mingmei's face.

She stared at the headless body still standing in front of her, then as it crumpled at her feet, she screamed.

75

John didn't hesitate. He turned, grabbed hold of Adriana and pulled her to the ground, throwing himself on top of her.

He could hear Mingmei screaming, and the panicked shouts of the guards, and behind that another noise, a rhythmic thump, thump, thump, and the hum of an engine. A helicopter.

"Stay down," he spoke into Adriana's hair, and then dared to raise his head and look around. The guards had all taken a knee and formed a perimeter. Six of them, all with their weapons raised to their shoulders, frantically scanning the horizon, trying to work out where the gunshot had come from. Steve lay face down in the gravel, blood running down the side of his face from a wound on the back of his head. He stirred, slowly raising his head. His eyes were unfocused, and small stones stuck to the blood on his cheek.

"Stay where you are, Steve," John hissed, hoping his friend wasn't too groggy to understand. Steve's eyes cleared, and he nodded, then winced as the movement sent pain shooting through his skull. John looked back over his shoulder. Mingmei was behind him, kneeling in the gravel beside Xie's headless body. She rocked back and forth, sobbing and pulling at her hair.

Then the guard on the far side of Mingmei toppled sideways into the gravel, twitched, and stopped moving.

Mingmei stopped her rocking and stared at the unmoving guard, then threw her head back and screamed so loudly it could be heard above the approaching helicopter. She ripped the SIG from Xie's hand, jumped to her feet, and rushed toward John.

A guard fell into the gravel between them, a neat hole in the middle of his forehead, and she stopped her headlong rush and planted her feet in the gravel. Snarling like a rabid dog, she raised the SIG in both hands and pointed it at his head.

John instinctively rolled sideways, pulling Adriana with him. There was an explosion of dust and gravel where John's head had been moments earlier, and then another, even closer. John scrabbled forward through the gravel toward another dead guard and yanked his sidearm free from its holster. Another bullet embedded itself in the ground beside him and he rolled onto his back, aimed between his feet and pulled the trigger, praying the weapon didn't have a safety. The first bullet went wide, embedding itself into the brick wall of the farmhouse. The second and third found their targets though, blotches of crimson blossoming in the front of Mingmei's blouse. She rocked on her feet, looking down in surprise, then her knees buckled and she fell to the ground.

He stared at her fallen body and slowly became aware of his surroundings again. Panicked shouting and gunfire and the roaring of a helicopter as a dark shape flew low overhead, sending dust and gravel flying.

He rolled back onto his stomach, ducked his head, covering his face, and scrambled backwards until he felt his feet bump up against Adriana. Opening his eyes, he was suddenly aware that the gunfire had ceased. The smell of propellant, hot gun-oil, jet fuel and the coppery scent of blood filled his nostrils, and though the shooting had stopped, there was a constant ringing in his ears. An eerie silence descended, broken only by the anguished groan of a wounded man. He dared to raise his head and look around. There was no-one left standing, the farmyard littered with bodies.

John slowly sat up. "Adriana are you ok?"

"*Sim,* yes, yes."

John was about to call out Steve's name when several shadowy figures materialised in the dawn light—clad in black, large goggles where the eyes should be, not an inch of human skin showing.

They advanced slowly, communicating by hand signal, automatic weapons held to their shoulders, the barrels following the movement of their heads. They spread out, eight of them, moving softly and silently like black panthers.

One stopped and nudged a body with his boot. The body groaned.

John heard a pfft, and the body jerked, and went silent.

A black boot appeared in his peripheral vision and he turned to see a black figure looking down at him, the muzzle of his weapon pointed at his head. John dropped the pistol into the gravel and clasped his hands behind his head, hoping these new arrivals wouldn't see him as a threat.

Hands grabbed him by the back of his collar and dragged him across the gravel, depositing him in the middle of the farmyard.

Steve was dragged beside him, followed by Adriana. They were lined up side by side, their hands clasped behind their heads as the figures in black stood guard.

"Who are these guys?" Steve whispered out of the side of his mouth.

John remained silent, watching them, trying to get a sense as to who they were. He recognized the weapons. He had seen Joseph Tamba and his men use them. MP5SDs, the suppressed version of the Heckler and Koch MP5, used by law enforcement all over the world. Was it the Portuguese? He wasn't sure, but something about their build seemed off. Even in their tactical clothing and load vests, their build seemed too small to be European.

"What do we do now?" The question came from Adriana, for the first time, a hint of fear audible in her voice.

John didn't know what to say. He wanted to reassure her, but he had no idea what was going on.

One man reached up and flipped his NVGs up onto his helmet and John saw his eyes for the first time.

Chinese.

His stomach churned, and he fought to gain control as his heart rate went through the roof.

The man walked over to Xie's body and looked down at him for several moments, then he crouched down beside Mingmei. He pulled off a glove and placed two fingers on the side of her neck. Feeling nothing, he got to his feet, allowed his MP5 to swing on its sling, and drew his sidearm. Walking back to John, he pointed at his head.

"Fuck me," Steve muttered. John steeled himself, pulling his shoulders back and looked the man straight in the eye.

"No, please don't," Adriana whimpered.

"It's okay, *meu amor*," John reassured her as his body trembled with fear. He unclasped his hands, lowered his arms to his side, and stuck his chin out in defiance. If this was the end, he was not going out like a coward.

The man stared back at him, then something changed in his eyes. He tilted his head slightly, as if listening intently, then took a step back and pressed a button on a device attached to his vest. He turned his head away, but John could see his lips moving, the sound only audible to his throat mike. After he stopped speaking, he turned back to face John. Studying him briefly, he gave a subtle nod. Then, he holstered his weapon and raised a hand, making a circular motion above his head.

The other men backed away, lowered their weapons and then melted away into the soft light of dawn.

76

Archie lowered his PVS-14 Night Vision Monocular and gave a satisfied nod. Everything had gone swimmingly.

Retrieving his phone from the dashboard, he pressed redial. It was answered immediately.

"Thank you Anson, old chap. You did the right thing. I'm sure you wouldn't have wanted to read about your illegal Chinese military operation in the Portuguese press. European governments can be a bit touchy about that sort of thing." He listened for a bit and then added, "No, no, don't you worry. I have a cleanup crew inbound as we speak. Leave it to me. Let's call this matter closed, shall we?"

He listened some more, nodded a couple of times as if Anson could see him, and then added, "You have my word, Anson. And my invitation to come up to the house for the weekend still stands. I'll call you when I get back. I'm sure Celia would love to see the rose garden."

Archie ended the call and grinned. He dropped the phone on the seat beside him and removed a thermos from the cup holder. Unscrewing the top, he took a sip of hot tea while watching the scene through his windshield. There was now enough light for him to see without the use of a night vision device and he could see John walking with his arm around Adriana toward the BMW. Steve followed a few steps behind.

Archie screwed the top back on the thermos and set it down. All in all a good morning's work.

John Hayes had done well. He was indeed a very resourceful man. In fact, Archie could go as far as to say he had a lot of potential... given the right training.

He leaned forward, pressed the start button and selected Drive. As the Jaguar SUV rolled up the track toward the farmhouse, Archie pondered the one question that remained unanswered.

Who shot Xie?

77

About five hundred metres to the east of the farmhouse, a mound of leaves stirred, then rose off the ground as it transformed into a large man dressed in a sniper's ghillie suit.

A second mound close to the first went through the same transformation.

"That was close," Joseph Tamba muttered, easing his finger from the trigger of the Barrett M82.

"That Chinaman will never know how lucky he was," Moses chuckled beside him. He pushed himself up to a kneeling position, brushing off the branches and leaves that had covered him only moments earlier. "That was an incredible shot, Sir."

"Thank you, Moses. But I can't take all the credit. Without you as a spotter, it would have been much more difficult."

Moses smiled shyly and began disassembling his spotter scope and packing it away.

Joseph gazed out across the fields toward the farmhouse. He could see John, Steve, and the woman he guessed to be

Adriana moving toward the X5 leaving a pile of bodies behind in the farmyard. John had handled himself well, but Joseph had expected nothing less. From their first meeting months ago, John had done nothing but impress him.

As far as he was concerned, this whole incident was a win-win situation. He had settled a debt, John had retrieved his girlfriend, and Xie's demise marked the end of a troubling chapter in Nkuru's history.

The woman's demise was an unexpected benefit. She was known to Joseph—no-one made enquiries in Nkuru without him finding out. But now she was gone, and he didn't have to worry about it.

Noticing movement along the track leading to the farmhouse, he lifted the Barrett off its tripod, and aimed at a green SUV inching up the track. Peering through the scope, he focused on the driver; a middle-aged man with floppy hair, dressed in a tweed suit. Joseph lowered the weapon. The man didn't appear threatening, and he was sure John could handle him.

He began dismantling the weapon and stowing it into its case. He wanted to return to the van and shed the ghillie suits before the world stirred to life.

78

John stood near the foot of the steps, a smile spreading across his face as he felt a warm glow inside.

At the top of the steps stood his parents, each holding onto a comically oversized pair of scissors. It had been Adriana's suggestion. She stood on the opposite side of the steps, radiant as ever, fastening the end of a wide red ribbon to the doorframe.

"Are you ready?" she called out, and the crowd of onlookers responded in unison, "Ready!"

His parents stepped forward and, with the oversized scissors, snipped the ribbon in two. A round of applause sprang up from the garden and Carole Hayes let go of the scissors to hug Adriana. She then turned and held up her hand, gesturing for quiet and once the applause had stopped, she beckoned for John to join her on the step.

"My wonderful son, John," she announced to the crowd. "It's because of him we are now back in our beautiful home. One that's even better than before."

John felt his cheeks flush as the crowd once more

applauded and then someone in the back called out, "speech, speech."

John couldn't see, but he knew by the accent who it was. Steve had arrived from Dubai that morning together with Maadhavi. He saw her now, beaming at him from the rear of the crowd.

Before he could speak, the pop of a champagne bottle filled the air, followed by another cheer from the crowd.

Waving for silence, he said, "I'd like to propose a toast, so please grab a glass."

As the champagne circulated through the crowd, Adriana joined him, passing glasses to him and his parents.

Raising his glass, John addressed the gathering. "It's unfair for me to take any credit for this. It's because of you, our friends, that we could do this."

He searched the crowd, looking for the faces he wanted. "Philip? Philip Symonds, where are you?"

"Here."

John smiled and raised the glass in his direction. "Phillip helped me deal with all the horrendous paperwork that goes with rebuilding a house of this age. I couldn't have done it without you. Thank you.

Will, Will Sanderson. Where are you?"

"Over here John."

John spotted him and again raised his glass in salute. "Will Sanderson, the best contractor in Hampshire. Thank you." John paused and looked down at his feet, composing his thoughts. He looked up, his eyes roaming the faces of his parents' friends and neighbors. "When mum and dad's house burnt down, it felt like the end of the world for me."

"And me," his dad piped up from beside him, prompting a laugh from the crowd.

"Yes," John grinned. "And you made sure I knew it."

The crowd laughed again.

"Someone wiser than me once said, 'when faced with adversity, remember the power of choice. Choose hope, choose strength, choose a brighter tomorrow.' And that's what my parents did. That's what all of you did. You supported them in their time of need and helped make this happen." John paused again. "Many of you may not be aware, but it was an act of arson that destroyed the house. But one man's evil act was the seed for something greater, something way more powerful. The expansion of love and community spirit." He raised his glass. "To all of you, thank you."

The group erupted in cheers and the clink of glasses.

"Well said, Son." David Hayes clinked his glass against John's. "I'm proud of you."

John felt a lump in his throat and he raised the glass to his lips, draining half of it in one go.

"I'm... ah... I'll just see to the guests, Dad."

John stepped down into the crowd, nodding and smiling at those he recognized and even those he didn't. He made his way over to a line of tables straining under the weight of food supplied by neighbors, and his mum's friends from the Womens' Institute. Sandwiches, quiches, cakes, cookies and scones. On another table were jugs of Pimms, and bottles of champagne in tubs filled with ice.

"Good speech."

"Thank you." John turned and just managed to hide his surprise. "Archibold Cholmondeley-Warner, I'm glad you could make it." Although John wasn't sure he had been invited.

"I was in the area, John. Thought I'd pop in and see what you've done with the place."

"Thank you. Champagne?"

"Don't mind if I do."

John grabbed a glass of champagne from the table and handed it to Archie, who was admiring the house. "I saw it after the fire, you know."

"Really? I didn't know that."

"Yes." Archie smiled, turned and clinked his glass against John's. "Chin-chin."

John nodded and took a sip of champagne.

"It's hard to believe this is the same property. You did well."

"Not me, Archie. You heard my speech."

"An army is only as good as its general, John."

John shrugged. He didn't feel comfortable taking any credit.

"Ms. D'Silva seems to have dealt with things well."

John gazed across the crowd at Adriana. She and Maadhavi had their heads together, giggling away about something. "She's a tough one."

"She is indeed. As are you, John. In fact, there's something I'd like to discuss with you when you have a bit more time."

John only half heard him, his attention drawn to a sound in the sky, one he was becoming all too familiar with. The rhythmic thump of a rotor and the whine of powerful engines. He spotted it approaching from the north-east, a helicopter, its nose pitching up as it decelerated and flared into a hover above the field opposite Willow Cottage.

"Excuse me one moment, Archie," John shouted above the noise but didn't wait for an answer, and pushed his way through the crowd and out onto the lane. The helicopter lowered into the field, the downwash kicking up a tornado of dust and debris before it settled onto the ground. It was a twin-engine AW139, white with a dark green diagonal stripe running across the cockpit. John recognized the coat of arms on the tail and he grinned.

Two large men jumped out and positioned themselves facing the cottage. Despite wearing suits, they were armed with MP5s.

The passenger door swung open, revealing a tall, slim black man. His hair was gray, and he was impeccably dressed in a finely tailored Prince of Wales check suit. Another, familiar, man climbed out behind him and they both walked toward John, escorted on either side by the armed men.

The noise level dropped as the helicopter powered down and John stepped forward and opened the gate in the wall of the field.

"Father, I would like to introduce a good friend of the Democratic Republic of Nkuru, Mr. John Hayes. John, my father, President Tamba."

President Tamba grasped John's hand in both of his. "Joseph has told me a lot about you. I can never thank you enough for what you've done for my country."

John blinked in surprise and glanced over his shoulder at Joseph, who was grinning widely.

"Thank you, Mr President."

"Oh no, please call me Baba."

It was Joseph's turn to look surprised, but he quickly composed himself. "My father wanted to meet your parents and bring them a little gift from Nkuru."

"Family is very important, John," Babatunde Tamba beamed at him. "But of course you know that. My son Joseph and I consider you part of the Nkuru family now."

"I'm honored."

Babatunde Tamba turned and beckoned to another man, who had joined them from the helicopter. The man walked over and handed over a box made of highly polished ebony. Embossed in gold on the lid was the Nkuru coat of arms. Babatunde took it from him and beamed at John. "Now, why don't you introduce me to your parents?"

John stepped aside to allow the delegation to exit the field. Curious guests filled the lane, but they parted as John guided Joseph's group through them toward the house.

As they walked past, Archie raised a glass, and called out, "President Tamba."

President Tamba paused, reached out and placed a hand on Archie's shoulder. "Archibold, what a pleasure."

John did a double-take, unsure if he had heard correctly. He frowned at Archibold, who winked and raised his glass again.

Confused, John escorted the President over to his parents, who were still standing on the steps of Willow Cottage.

"Mum, Dad, I'd like you to meet the President of Nkuru, President Tamba," John made the introductions to his stunned parents.

They blinked but didn't reply, their mouths hanging open.

Babatunde Tamba stepped forward, rescuing them by handing a wooden box to Carole Hayes. "I wanted to bring you a housewarming gift," he explained.

Carole blushed and curtsied. Babatunde then extended his hand to David Hayes. "You should be very proud of your son, Mr. Hayes," he said.

David regained his composure. "Thank you." He cleared his throat. "I am proud of him."

John felt his cheeks flush and attempted to change the subject. "Why don't you open the box, Mum?" he suggested.

"Of course," Carole giggled, passing the box to David. He

held it for her as she flicked open the catches and lifted the lid.

"Oh, how lovely," John's mum exclaimed.

Looking over her shoulder, John felt the blood drain from his face.

Inside the box was a *Jiu Choi Maau*.

A Chinese cat.

ALSO BY MARK DAVID ABBOTT

For a complete list of all my books please visit my website: www.markdavidabbott.com

The John Hayes Series

Vengeance: John Hayes #1

A Million Reasons: John Hayes #2

A New Beginning: John Hayes #3

No Escape: John Hayes #4

Reprisal: John Hayes #5

Payback: John Hayes #6

The Guru: John Hayes #7

Faith: John Hayes #8

The neighbor: John Hayes #9

The Chinese Cat: John Hayes #10

The John Hayes Bundles

The John Hayes Thrillers Bundle #1 : Books 1-3

The John Hayes Thrillers Bundle #2 : Books 4-6

The John Hayes Thrillers Bundle #3 : Books 7-9

The Max Jones Series

The Mule: Max Jones #1

The Irishman: Max Jones #2

The Hong Kong Series

Disruption: Hong Kong #1

Conflict: Hong Kong #2

Freedom: Hong Kong #3

The Hong Kong Series Bundle: Books 1-3

The Devil Inside Duology

The Devil Inside

Flipped

The Devil Inside : Bundle

As M D Abbott

Once Upon A Time In Sri Lanka

ENJOYED THIS BOOK? YOU CAN MAKE A BIG DIFFERENCE.

First of all thank you so much for taking the time to read my work. If you enjoyed it, then I would be extremely grateful if you would consider leaving a short review for me on your store of choice. A good review means so much to every writer but especially to self-published writers like myself. It helps new readers discover my books and allows me more time to create stories for you to enjoy.

ABOUT THE AUTHOR

Mark can be found online at:
www.markdavidabbott.com

on Facebook
www.facebook.com/markdavidabbottauthor

on Instagram
www.instagram.com/markdavidabbottauthor

or on email at:
www.markdavidabbott.com/contact